An Honest

Dragon

AN ELUSIVE DRAGON

Dragons of Mayfair Book 2

E.B. WHEELER

Rowan Ridge
Press

Print ISBN: 978-1-7360411-2-3

First printing: November 2021

Published by Rowan Ridge Press, Utah

Cover and interior design © Rowan Ridge Press

Front cover image by Onesketchman based on "Portrait of Doña Antonia Zárate" by Francisco Goya

Back cover image "Cobb Gate, Lyme Regis" by Reed

❀ Created with Vellum

For everyone who needs a little magic
in their lives

Chapter One

ELIZA PRESCOTT, dragon-linked West Indies heiress, planned to engage herself to the most abominable man possible.

"I really don't see any other way," she said to Phoebe Hart—No, it was Lady Phoebe Westing now that her friend was married.

The waters of the English Channel lapped hungrily at the women's bare feet as they walked the dark line in the sand left by the sea. Phoebe and the Viscount of Westing had retreated to Dorset for their wedding instead of marrying in London in order to avoid the notice of the anti-magic Luddites. Those revolutionaries, who wanted to rid Britain of dragons and the magic they brought to their bonded humans, would have loved the opportunity to attack the wedding of two such dragon-linked people. Phoebe said it only mattered that she and Westing were together.

Eliza was glad for her friend and only a little envious, fearing that she had little chance for such a happy match. She huffed. "Father is completely unreasonable."

Phoebe kept a hand on her bonnet so the salty wind didn't steal it away. "But you wouldn't marry someone awful just to spite your father."

"Oh, I don't actually have to marry the man." Eliza side-stepped the foaming swash of a broken wave. The tide was coming in, and she didn't want to ruin her white muslin. "Father just has to *think* I will. It can't be just any scoundrel, though. It has to be someone he can't actually object to. A lord would be best. That's what he wants for me: a marriage to some influential nobleman or politician. But once he sees how terrible it would be for my fortune to go to some empty-headed dandy, he'll finally let me manage my own affairs."

Phoebe stopped and frowned, idly watching as Mushroom, her dragon, played with Eliza's dragon Amethyst in the waves. "If he cares enough not to see you in a miserable marriage, he must care enough to let you have your freedom if you just explain it to him."

"He thinks women are too silly to do anything on their own. He has no idea just how silly men can be. If he saw the men in London…" She rolled her eyes. "Not that he's likely to leave Dominica. Oh, but of course Lord Westing isn't silly. You were fortunate enough to get one of the good men. Didn't leave as much for the rest of us to scrabble over."

Phoebe flushed and looked up the shoreline where her husband, obvious by his white-blond hair, stood in conversation with her brother Max. "He is good. And definitely not silly. Though I own there are some very silly men. Still, it seems unfair to toy with them."

Eliza had a bit of hesitation over that idea as well. "I will make sure not to entangle myself with anyone who actually cares about me. Not that there are many. My fortune is my biggest appeal, I'm afraid. And my dragon, of course."

"No!" Phoebe looked sincerely shocked. "You have many dear qualities."

Eliza smiled. "And kindness is among yours. But anyone who is only interested in my magic or my fortune deserves to learn a lesson."

Phoebe bit her lip, her brow drawn in concern, but she didn't argue. Both ladies stared off at the never-ending waves rolling toward them. The autumn sun warmed Eliza's skin, but the deep, cold waters lapped against her thoughts as relentless as the tides, its slithery voice full of bones and forgotten treasures grasped by dark, unfeeling currents. It called her closer.

Amethyst bounded over and jumped to Eliza's shoulder as if

sensing her unease. Eliza put her hand on the reassuring warmth of the dusky purple dragon, and the creature rubbed its head against her fingers. The sea was not her lord and master. She was the one with water magic—she would not let *it* control *her*.

"Gathering wool, love?"

The voice of her trustee, Captain Parry, drew her back like a rope hauling her from the waves. Phoebe discreetly wandered away. Eliza wished she wouldn't be so polite.

Captain Parry gave her one of his bright grins, and the eye that wasn't covered by a black patch twinkled with charm. Oh yes, this man—not more than seven years older than herself—was the person her father thought more responsible than she was. The sea wind teased her black curls, tangling them with a stray ribbon from her bonnet, and she brushed both out of her face.

"We travel all this distance to visit Westing Hall," he said, "and now you look like you're a thousand miles away."

She put on a too-sweet smile. "*You* need not have traveled at all. Phoebe—*Lady Westing*—would have been a perfectly acceptable chaperone."

"Then what would you have done when you ran out of pin money and wanted some pretty new bauble?" His words sparkled with amusement.

"You could simply let me have the management of my money. My father need not know."

He put on an expression of mock seriousness, though his lips still curled in a smile. "But what kind of trouble might you get into without my wisdom guiding you?"

"I might actually succeed in situating myself in society."

"What, marry some *dull* lord and spend your life going to *dull* parties? No, we cannot have that."

"At least I would not have anyone managing me."

"Ah, then it's a stupid, old lord you have your heart set on? One too doddering to know or care what you do, as long as you spoon feed him his soup every night?"

Eliza wrinkled her nose at the thought, but she lifted her chin. "If that is what I want, it's no affair of yours."

"Oh, but it is, love. I'm your trustee, after all."

Eliza looked away from his gray stare. She never knew what to make of his mercurial moods, too much like the whims of the sea. Amethyst flicked her tail, mirroring Eliza's annoyance. "You are a tyrant."

"I know how to run a neat ship."

"I'm not one of your crew!"

He grinned, wolf-like. "More's the pity."

"I would mutiny," she growled.

"What a darling challenge you would be."

Eliza huffed. "Leave me alone."

"Since you ask so kindly…" He gave a mock little bow and strolled off to look for shells or pebbles in the surf.

"Impossible!" Eliza muttered to Amethyst.

Captain Parry was the one thing holding her back. He could be amusing, even reassuring at times, but she wished her father had not given him control of her finances while she was in England. Between the inheritance left by her mother and her allowance from her father, Eliza should have had enough money to enjoy herself. But Parry was as strict as any navy quartermaster. He scolded her for spending too much on a box at the opera so she could mingle with the most fashionable people. He would not let her have her own mare in London to ride out in Hyde Park and meet the eligible gentlemen of the *haut ton*. He even frowned when she bought Miss Charity's latest book so she could gossip about it with her friends. It was almost as if he didn't want her to be a social success.

She only had a moment to fume at him before Joshua and Alexandria, Lord Westing's young half-siblings, ran up to her.

"Miss Prescott! Will you make the water dance again? Please?" Joshua gestured to the trickle of water flowing down the cliff to the shore.

Alexandria grinned around the thumb stuck in her mouth.

"Of course," Eliza said, smiling at their hopeful expressions.

They had built a little network of ponds and canals in the sand to collect the water and sail their toy boats. Their mother, Lady Zoe, the dowager viscountess, had used her dragon-linked attunement to air to create breezes to push the boats around. Now, however, Lady Zoe watched the sea, no doubt missing her home in Greece, and the rising tide nibbled away at the edges of the children's creation. That was the way of the sea.

Amethyst hopped down to trot along the beach, stopping to dig a shell out of the sand and carry it carefully between her sharp teeth. Another treasure for her hoard. Like Eliza, she liked pretty baubles. *And there was nothing wrong with that*, Eliza mentally scolded Captain Parry.

The children stopped well back from the dark cliff face, aware of how common mudslides were along the Dorset coast.

Eliza turned her attention to the trickle of water. Its energy hummed through her, glad to be moving and free. Water disliked being contained. She understood. She reached out a hand and called to the water. It interrupted its downward flow to swirl and jump in the air. It caught the sunlight and sparkled with the brilliance of the finest crystal chandelier before falling to the ground like rain drops.

Joshua laughed and reached out to catch the drops as they fell.

But where was Alexandria?

Eliza quickly scanned the shore. The little girl toddled through the uprush of the waves, her arms out for balance. The sea had stolen the girl's boat, and she had wandered into the surf to fetch it, heedless of the rising swells heading toward her.

Eliza's throat tightened, and she rushed forward. "Alexandria!"

Lady Zoe looked over, her eyes wide with alarm. Phoebe and Lord Westing, who strolled down the beach in the blissful obliviousness of the newly married, turned back. But they were all too far away. Eliza was closest. She ran into the waves, but they pushed at her as if determined to keep her from the child. Eliza hiked up her skirts and strode forward, the icy water sucking at her. The sea wanted her, wanted her, wanted her.

A wave slammed into Alexandria, knocking her under.

Eliza froze in horror.

Captain Parry surged ahead of her. Unhampered even by his false leg, he splashed over to grab the girl's dress floating like a jellyfish on the water and hauled her out.

Lady Zoe, who had caught up with Eliza, shrieked and sloshed forward. Parry pushed past her, bringing the child to shore and laying her on her side to pound her back. Alexandria coughed and choked, spitting up sea water.

Lady Zoe gasped and gathered her child up in her arms. "Never, ever do that again, my love!"

"I wanted my boat," Alexandria rasped out.

Eliza looked down at the waves slurping around her feet. The toy boat knocked against her, as if the sea were returning it in penance. She snatched it up before the waves could change their mind.

She sloshed out of the water and handed the child the boat.

"Thank you," Alexandria said meekly.

Her words were lost under her mother's effusive praise for Captain Parry, which he shrugged off.

"I was closest," he said.

But that wasn't true. Eliza had been closer. She had failed the little girl. She shrank back from the group gathered around Alexandria.

Parry casually slipped away from the others to stand near her. Eliza didn't know what he wanted. Congratulations? Thanks for covering for her mistake? To tease her for being a coward?

Amethyst flapped from her shoulder to Parry's, landing on the side with his good eye and butting his chin. He smiled and scratched the dragon between her wings.

"I suppose now you have everyone singing your praises," Eliza said.

He raised an eyebrow. "Not everyone, love."

She flushed and looked down at the damp sand. Little pock marks formed where the water dripped from her ruined gown. "I am glad you were there to save her. I could not do it."

"It would be no easy task to command the waves of the sea."

Eliza looked at him, startled. She hadn't even thought of trying to use her magic against the sea's might. Is that what everyone thought she had attempted? She felt foolish, but she would not correct him, because it was even more foolish that she had just stood there in terror of walking into the waves when she sensed all the force of the sea behind them.

"Don't worry," Parry said in a stage whisper. "I'll even give you the funds to buy a new dress."

She glowered. Amethyst glided back to her shoulder, and Parry laughed and wandered away.

Joshua skipped over to Eliza. "Thank you for saving my sister's boat, Miss Prescott." His eyes glowed with admiration as he took in her dragon. "Will you come play with us? Alexandria is feeling better now."

Phoebe stepped in. "I think our outing is over for today, Josh. Everyone is tired and over-excited."

He sighed in resignation and went to retrieve his own boat.

Phoebe gave Eliza a look of mock solemnity. "Next time, we will try to invite some gentlemen slightly older than Joshua to entertain you."

Eliza laughed. "Joshua is quite entertaining." She did need to meet some eligible gentlemen, however. Actually, not so much eligible gentlemen as puffed-up coxcombs. The kind her father would especially dislike.

"And you always have Captain Parry," Phoebe said, a sparkle in her eyes.

Eliza rolled her eyes. "Don't remind me! I think he was bored in London, too."

"Hmm."

Eliza shot Phoebe a suspicious look. Whatever her friend was thinking, Eliza should put an end to her schemes. Captain Parry was handsome, true enough, but he was also arrogant and delighted in vexing Eliza. And he was not a lord. Eliza didn't care so much about the title, but the freedom that came with it, that was what she craved.

"Captain Parry is nothing but a determined flirt," Eliza said. "And he's as bad as my father. It's his management I'm trying to get away from, remember."

"Of course," Phoebe said, sounding a little sad.

Eliza suppressed a sigh. Sometimes, Phoebe might be too sweet for her own good. Or for Eliza's.

As everyone traipsed back up the cliffside trail to Westing's estates, Eliza lagged behind, still tired and embarrassed from her failure to save Alexandria. She felt something like a tickle in the back of her mind. A distant whisper.

Danger.

She gave a start and looked around. Of course, no one had spoken. It was only her and Amethyst. Yet the voice had been as clear as if someone had been sitting beside her. Was this some message from the sea? She shivered and hurried to catch up with the others.

Chapter Two

WESTING HALL WAS, in Lord Westing's words, an architectural disaster. His recent ancestors, in chasing design trends, had created an estate for themselves that reminded Eliza of the mishmash sandcastle the children might have created if they were attuned to earth. The main wing was blocky with tall Greek columns flanking the entrance like footmen, but a newer wing had a dome with many round windows that gawped at its more formal counterpart like a drunken fop with too many quizzing glasses. The inside was a wild Rococo mish-mash of arching ceilings and entrance ways all painted white and pastel and decorated with plaster vines, dragons jumping through gold-leafed waves, and bare-bottomed cherubim frolicking amongst clouds overhead. The airy brightness suited Phoebe, but not as much Westing, who was attuned to ice. Still, it was his ancestral home, and he did not change it.

Eliza's room had plasterwork shells all around the windows, which looked out toward the sea. She wondered if Phoebe had chosen it for her intentionally. The setting sun flashed off the distant waves, and she quickly looked away. The draw and push of the tides moved in a secret spot in her chest, like she always had to fight to keep herself steady. She would have chosen a different element, given a choice—maybe light, like Phoebe, or wind, carefree and always on the move. The sea had taught her early that it was no friend of hers. It would toss her aside with as little feeling as any other tiny human. Whomever she married would have to have an estate far from the shore.

She watched dusk gather across the landscape created by Capability Brown, the famous designer attuned to plants—as Westing had told them with more pride than he would admit to feeling for the house. It all looked natural, right down to the false ruins teetering along the cliffs. From the vantage of the house, Eliza detected a pattern in the planting of trees and meadow, drawing her attention to a tor jutting above where the rolling green hills ended in a sudden plunge to the sea below.

Amethyst dropped her new shell into her hoard with the other pebbles and baubles she had collected from lakes and beaches. She trotted over to sniff at the salty air drifting in from the open window.

"Does it make you homesick?" Eliza asked, stroking the dragon's head. "I miss the West Indies, too, sometimes, but this is where we must make our home." If she lived too close to her father, he would smother her with his own ideas of what a young lady wanted. He meant well, she supposed, but she often wondered if the gifts and parties were more about him showing off his dragon-linked daughter than any consideration of what she actually desired. No, her only chance at being able to breathe free was to make a life for herself in England. That meant a good marriage. Hopefully not to an idiot, but if engaging herself to such a man bought her some freedom, then so be it. "Would you rather be in London?"

Amethyst yawned, showing a row of sharp teeth.

"You're right," Eliza said. "London is dull now that the Season is over."

And when London wasn't dull, it was dangerous. Shaw and his anti-magic Luddites were still out there, hoping to eliminate the dragon-linked from England as Napoleon's revolutionary forces did in Europe.

Eliza sighed and gazed out the window with her dragon. The false ruins on the cliff edge were in danger of being swept down by a mudslide someday, but they did look charming silhouetted by the gathering dark. Amethyst's head perked up, and she made a clicking noise in her throat. A light glinted among the columns. Eliza strained to see if it was some trick of design or magic. But no, it moved like a person carrying a lantern. The light winked out then flashed a couple of times. The signal was answered by one farther out to sea.

Eliza stiffened and squinted into the darkness. Perhaps it was just a local fisherman, but she was from the West Indies: she knew something of the world of pirates and smugglers, and she did not think the scene on the cliffs was innocent. Worse than smugglers, it might be wreckers, hoping to lure hapless ships into dangerous waters to claim their treasures. Her chest tightened, and she pressed her fingers against the cold plaster of the windowsill.

Someone tapped on the door. Eliza gave a start and hurried to open the door.

Parry stood there in his evening dress, which looked a little incongruous with his wooden leg and eye patch. Amethyst hopped to Eliza's shoulder and flicked her tongue at him.

"And I'm overjoyed to see you, too, my scaly beauty," he said, bowing to the dragon.

Amethyst regarded him with interest, then flapped her wings and glided over to Parry's shoulder. He replaced his hat and grinned at Eliza. "Ready to dine?"

Eliza glanced back at the window. "I think I saw something out there on the water. Smugglers or wreckers. Come see."

Parry looked sharply at the window and took a step forward. But he paused at the threshold of the door, like it had some power to hold him outside of her chambers, and shook his head. "You need to tell Westing."

"You would know better than he would what trouble it might mean."

"It's his district, and he understands it best. Besides, it is improper for you to invite a gentleman into your room."

She rolled her eyes. "It's only you."

His jaw tightened in the stubborn way that meant it was no use arguing with him. "Warn our host and leave it to him. You don't have to manage everything on your own."

"Well, I refuse to leave it all to luck." She huffed and walked past him toward the grand staircase.

Tom, the cat Phoebe had rescued and pressed on Westing, trotted along beside Eliza as if escorting her to where Phoebe waited at the top of the stairs.

"I hope you don't dine so late on our account," Eliza said.

Phoebe grinned. "Country hours, you mean? We haven't yet adjusted to them. It's a luxury to be able to sleep in. And to think, not many months ago I never would have dreamed in staying in bed so late." She flushed and quickly said, "You must be hungry, though."

"Famished," Parry assured her, coming up behind Eliza. "But not as famished as I am for the sight of you lovely ladies."

"Careful," Phoebe said with a laugh. "Westing won't hesitate to call you out."

"I'm not such a bad shot myself," Parry said, strolling ahead of them. "Even with the one eye."

Phoebe laughed again.

"You shouldn't encourage him," Eliza said.

"Are you afraid he'll really get in a duel?" Phoebe teased, walking Eliza down to the dining room.

Eliza chuckled. "Perhaps. And if you make his head too big, he'll be an easy target."

Phoebe laughed easily. She looked happy, and Eliza was happy for her. It seemed a good omen. Eliza had done right to leave London behind for a time. And perhaps being near the sea would be good for her—let her put its influence aside once and for all.

"I hope you will not find it dull here," Phoebe said. "There are a few neighbors we dine with, and with Lyme nearby and the London Season over, 'friends' from town are always stopping in for dinner. Especially single young men."

"Oh, I imagine!" Eliza laughed at the mental image of a trail of hungry bachelors lining up for a free meal.

"We have another sort of guest tonight. A, uh, lonely neighbor who often stops by unannounced." Phoebe looked like she wanted to say more but couldn't find polite words.

Eliza, her curiosity piqued, wondered what horrors awaited her at the dinner table.

Westing joined them, and Eliza remembered what she had seen out her window. "There was something I wanted to mention to you both."

Westing looked somber, as usual. "What's wrong?"

"I saw a light flashing out on the cliff. I wondered… I thought of wreckers."

His face settled into a serious frown. "Wreckers usually wouldn't dare, but even if it's smugglers, they're being very bold. Thank you for telling me. I'll send someone down to investigate."

Eliza nodded and let Phoebe's brother Max escort her to the table. Normally a lively young man, his face was drawn down in a long frown. Eliza wondered if it had anything to do with the lonely neighbor—which must be the identity of the bony old woman with the tremendous hooked nose and the tremendous glitter of jewels about her person. The lady pursed her lips and glared at everyone in such a way that she might sour any cheerful gentleman.

Captain Parry, by virtue of his military rank, had the dubious honor of taking the lady into dinner. The woman was not tall, but neither was Parry, and she looked over his various battle wounds as if evaluating his worthiness. Parry kept his expression politely blank. The lady took his arm only with hesitation, like she was afraid he would tarnish her silver bangles. Eliza glowered at the woman.

"She had best be careful with those jewels," Eliza whispered to Max, "or one of the dragons might try to steal her for its hoard."

He rewarded her with a glimmer of a smile, but it faded quickly.

"Lady Sophie," Westing said. "You have met Captain Nathaniel Parry. May I introduce our other guest, Miss Elizabeth Prescott. Lady Sophie Harcort is our neighbor."

Lady Sophie settled her scrutiny on Eliza, taking in her brown skin and curly black hair.

"Jamaica," Lady Sophie said decisively.

"Dominica," Eliza responded, trying not to smirk in satisfaction at correcting the haughty woman.

Lady Sophie squinted a little, as if trying to look deeper into Eliza. "You are wealthy. An heiress. Sugar?"

"Coffee," Eliza corrected.

Lady Sophie sniffed. "I don't care for coffee."

Eliza smiled sweetly. "Neither do I." Especially not after seeing the plantations where it was grown. "Nasty, bitter stuff."

Lady Sophie barked out a laugh. "Like me, you're thinking, eh? Well, you're right. I'm an irritable old woman. I frighten away poor Lady Zoe, so she won't dine with us tonight, but then the numbers would have been uneven anyway. Young Westing only invites me to dinner out of charity. And because we are distant cousins."

"Not at all," Westing said. "You keep everyone on their toes."

"I do! I have no patience for pretenses. I'm too old to have any kind of patience. You are attuned to water, though—that much I am sure of."

"You are right," Eliza conceded with a smile.

"Yes. I can see the blue in your dragon's sheen. That means water." She gestured to Captain Parry. "You will entertain me with tales of sea battles. This young man," she motioned to Max, "is too sulky to be good dinner company."

Max started and looked abashed. Eliza felt sorry for him, being picked at by a vulture.

Lady Sophie sipped her wine. "Too warm! Westing, chill it for me."

Westing raised an eyebrow but extended his hand for her drink. He held it up, and frost laced its way up the glass. He returned it with a smirk.

Lady Sophie quickly set the icy glass down. "You are a saucy young man! But at least it will not be too warm again."

As Lady Sophie predicted—or perhaps demanded—Captain Parry passed the dinner hour with tales of fighting the French at sea. Much exaggerated, Eliza suspected. Still, she was enjoying herself by the time the servants brought out the fruit and cream at the end of the meal.

Lady Sophie excused herself as soon as the meal was over.

"I have visitors arriving soon, so I don't want to tire myself out." She stated this like she was announcing that she had found fleas in her sheets. "I will expect you to come to dine with me while they are here. I will miss sensible company."

Westing raised an eyebrow. "Of course."

She nodded and shuffled off to call for her coachman.

Phoebe and Eliza prepared to withdraw as well and leave the men to their drinks. Before they made it to the door, however, a lad whom Eliza recognized from London, the street urchin called 'Brainy Jamie' whom Phoebe had taken under her wing, rushed into the room, his disreputable brown hair spiked in every direction.

"My lord! Come quickly!"

Westing rose instantly from the table. "What is it?"

Jamie gestured wildly behind him. "There's a boat in trouble on the waters, sir."

Chapter Three

WESTING HURRIED from the dining room, his dragon clinging to his shoulder and Jamie trotting along behind him. Max and Captain Parry exchanged glances and followed in his wake.

Phoebe stood as well, clutching her hands to her chest. "This part I can never get used to. The dangers of the sea. It frightens me."

Eliza nodded. "It is a powerful force."

Phoebe met her gaze, eyes wide. "Do you think we can help? With our attunements?"

Eliza thought about shipwrecks she had seen. "Perhaps. If there are any injured."

Phoebe's face darkened a little. "If there are wreckers, they will try to kill the survivors so they can claim the cargo."

"You think it's too dangerous?"

"I think we need to hurry."

The two women followed the path the men had taken out toward the cliffs. They didn't stop for a lantern. Phoebe held her hand out, and a glowing light formed, bobbing along in front of her like a well-trained hound. Eliza felt the immense power of the sea and shivered at the image of men trapped in its grasp.

Phoebe did not lead them down to the coast, but instead to a rise in the cliffs near the false ruins. Somewhere close to where Eliza had seen the light. She looked around, but they were alone as far as she could tell.

The cloudless sky showed no moon or stars, and the waves thundered against the cliffs in the darkness below. High tide had reclaimed the beach where they had strolled that afternoon.

"I can't see anything," Phoebe said.

She concentrated, and her light grew brighter, almost as bright as day. Eliza shielded her eyes. The figures of the men on the path below all turned for a moment in their direction then hurried down toward the treacherous black waters. Phoebe would not be able to maintain that much light for long, but Eliza could help Phoebe back to the house if she exhausted herself beyond walking.

In the meantime, Eliza scanned the water. The struggling rowboat stood out in silhouette, a solid form in the churning madness of the waves. The sea tossed it around like a toy. There was at least one form inside it, but Eliza couldn't tell if the person was rowing or if they were at the mercy of the waves. She closed her eyes, trying to feel the rhythm of the currents. If she could only give them a tiny nudge, she might move the boat closer to shore.

But in the angry hissing of the surf, she sensed that deep, timeless power. She pushed against it, but it swirled back to swallow her. She heard once again the nightmarish howl of hurricane winds tearing over Dominica, ripping houses and trees from the ground like a spoiled child throwing a tantrum. And the water, rising all around her, impossible for her to push aside. It was too much. Too strong. The sea always was.

She gasped and opened her eyes again, tearing herself away from the water's grip. Her head spun and her stomach heaved like she had been on a sea-tossed boat herself.

Phoebe's light was beginning to fade, but the men had splashed out into the ferocious waves to snag the rowboat from the grasp of the sea before it was dashed to bits against the great cliffs. The sight of them sent another wave of vertigo over Eliza, and she looked to Phoebe instead, who was pale and strained.

"They've almost got it to shore," Eliza said encouragingly.

Phoebe nodded faintly, still concentrating on the light. Captain Parry was out in the water with the boat now, the waves foaming about him, and Eliza wondered for a mad moment how he could possibly keep his balance with only one good leg to hold him upright. He seemed to be moving with the water, half swimming the boat along, until Max and Westing could grab the bow and pulled it onto the narrow strip of rocky shore visible while the tide was high.

"They have it!" Eliza called.

Phoebe sighed and lowered her arms, swaying on her feet. Eliza quickly caught her, afraid she was going to sag to the ground, but Phoebe managed to stay upright.

"Did they save him?" she asked.

"They got the boat to shore. I couldn't tell anything about the person in it."

"Let me rest a moment, and we'll see if they need help tending any injuries."

Eliza helped Phoebe sit on the damp grass. Mushroom curled up on her lap and rested his head on her chin with a deep sigh. They listened in the dark to the distant voices of the men, muffled by the pounding of the surf. Finally, Phoebe pushed herself up and summoned a faint light. Her cheeks still looked a bit washed out, but her eyes were alert.

"Let's go," she said.

They followed the path down the cliffside, Mushroom riding Phoebe's shoulder and Amethyst bounding ahead of them. A lantern glow drown out Phoebe's thin light, and Max approached, trudging back up from the beach.

"Max!" Phoebe called. "What happened? Did you save them?"

Max's face was pale, and he glanced back and forth between the women and the beach below. "Here's the thing, Phoebs. What you did with the light was great. A real help. But nothing would have done those men a bit of good. They were… already dead."

Eliza stiffened. "Already dead? There were bodies in the boat and no living people?"

"They, uh, had their throats cut."

"A boat full of men with their throats cut?" Phoebe gasped, going white again.

"Well, just two men, but yes, definitely cut. Not a pretty sight."

Westing and Captain Parry came up behind him, their faces grim.

"Is it true?" Eliza asked, raising her voice to be heard over the waters. "Someone killed two men and set them adrift?"

Max didn't look offended that Eliza questioned his account. He kept a comforting hand on his sister's arm and his face turned away from the beach.

"It looks that way," Westing said. "I'll raise the hue and cry tonight, and we'll try to find out what happened to them, and if anyone knows who they are. They might have run afoul of smugglers. Been left as a warning."

"I thought the smugglers were relatively harmless," Phoebe said.

"They usually are," Westing put an arm around her shoulder, drawing her away from her brother, and kissed her forehead. "Something unusual is going on here, but I will get to the bottom of it, and we'll see the scoundrels responsible punished."

Eliza glanced at Parry, who stood behind Westing. The lantern cast a shadow on his face, but his stern countenance looked foreboding in the strange light, and it made Eliza shiver.

The waves seemed to whisper something to her, but she turned her back on the cold breeze and hurried up the path back toward the house without trying to listen.

Parry took a glass of brandy in the library while Westing answered the ladies' questions and sent them off to bed. They had pulled the boat and the bodies a safe distance up the rocky shore, out of the way of the grasping waves, but otherwise left everything as it was for the justice of the peace and the coroner. Parry didn't want to think himself a coward, but the faces of the dead men stirred up too many ghosts, and he didn't want to mingle past and present. Instead, he stared out into the night and drank to the souls of the departed—recently and from years before—that they might find the peace in the next life that they were denied in this one.

Westing came in quietly, but Parry was still aware of the footsteps behind him, muffled as they were by soft rugs. He steeled himself to meet the present and turned to face his host.

"Bad business," Parry said.

Westing nodded once, his face grim as he stared into the cold fireplace.

Of course, he always looked grim. Not the most cheerful fellow Parry had known. But no one wanted an ugly mess like this to wash up on their shores—literally or figuratively.

"Not the normal work of smugglers," Parry pressed. "It's easy enough to sink a body in the sea. Someone wanted us to know they had killed these men."

Westing sighed and pushed his hand through his white-blond hair. "I know it. We received the message, but we don't know what it means."

"It might not have been meant for us," Parry said.

"I don't find that any more comforting," Westing almost snapped.

Not the best time to discuss the problem, then. Parry returned to his brandy and his brooding.

Westing had sent young Jamie to Lyme Regis for one of the justices of the peace as soon as they saw the bodies, and it was less than an hour after they settled in the library when Baxter, Westing's butler, showed a wind-blown gentleman in to see them.

"Ah, Mr. Blanding," Westing said, rising to greet the magistrate.

"My lord!" Blanding bowed. "What a dreadful thing!"

"Yes, that's why I sent for you directly instead of a constable. You've seen the bodies, then?" Westing asked.

"I have." Blanding turned his hat round and round in his hands.

"What do you think?"

"They haven't been dead long. The coroner took them away for closer inspection, but I think the cause of death is clear."

"Were they set loose from some ship?" Parry asked.

"I doubt it." The hat made another circuit. "At least one of them is a local boy."

"A known smuggler?" Westing asked.

"That's the thing that's worrisome, my lord. I can't say for sure who smuggles and who doesn't, of course, but he's got a reputation as an honest fisherman."

They were silent for a few heartbeats as they digested that information.

"Too honest, maybe?" Westing asked. "Came across someone who didn't want to be disturbed?"

"Could be," Blanding said. "We'll know more when we talk to the family and find out about the other lad."

Parry didn't envy Mr. Blanding the role of informing the family of their loss.

Westing bid the magistrate good night and Parry took the hint to retire to his room as well. He was haunted by the thought of an honest seafaring man cut down for his integrity, and even more so knowing the villain was still at large. Walking through the dark corridors of Westing Hall, Parry saw a new menace in the family portraits and cherubim adorning the walls, like everything around him was holding back secrets. The uneven step-thunk of his own stride, which he had grown used to since he lost his leg, set an eerie echo off the high ceilings. Give him a cozy ship's quarters over a sprawling pile like this anytime. The ship was easier to manage.

He paused outside Eliza's room. Speak of difficult to manage. He smiled to himself. He liked to see a lass with some backbone. As bold a face as she showed the world, Parry knew her well enough to see her unease, being always on display and always on guard. She liked the fine gowns and glittering jewels well enough, but he sensed a longing in her to be free. A longing he understood and wished he could answer.

Parry was her guardian, though, as he often had to remind himself. It was his job to keep her safe. Sometimes even from herself. She had grown up in a big house and probably wanted an estate like this one. She deserved it, too, if it would make her happy. But not at the cost of marrying an empty-headed ninny who didn't know how to appreciate her. Who would keep her in a cage like a canary on display. That, at least, Parry could do his upmost to prevent.

With a little bow to her chamber door, he went on his way to bed.

Chapter Four

ELIZA WOKE late in the morning, hoping to find the fishing boat and its dead sailors had only been a nightmare. But the somber faces that met her at the breakfast table told her she hadn't dreamed any of it.

"Any word from the justice of the peace?" Phoebe asked her husband, giving voice to Eliza's curiosity.

Mushroom ate a piece of ham on the table while Phoebe stroked his back. Westing's dragon, who bore the uninspired name of Dragon, watched for the chance to snatch some of it from his scaly housemate.

Westing prodded the eggs around his plate. "Mr. Blanding came up from Lyme. He recognized one of the boys as a local. Not a known smuggler. His companion is a stranger so far."

"Oh no." Phoebe set down her fork, staring unseeing at her plate. "The poor boy's family."

Eliza looked around the table. "What can we do?"

Westing sighed. "I've arranged for food to be brought to the family. I doubt they would appreciate a visit just now."

"The best thing we can do," Parry said quietly, "Is to find whomever is responsible."

Westing nodded.

"We'll have to go to Lyme," Phoebe announced. "We might hear something useful."

Eliza sensed the Earl of Blackerby's influence in that decision. The Secretary of the Home Office, attuned to shadow, was always scheming something or another, like a very well-dressed spider, and in the past, he had drawn both the Westings into his web.

"And get some shopping done, too?" Parry said with a slight smile at Eliza.

She ignored his teasing and focused on Phoebe. "It's a pleasant place, I understand."

"It is!" Phoebe's expression brightened. "There will be no assembly tonight since those are only Tuesday and Thursday, but we can see the seawall and the fossils. Those will interest you."

Westing raised an eyebrow. "You say that because they interest you."

"Of course!" Phoebe beamed. "And since I know Eliza has excellent taste, she will like them as well. West thinks they are dull," she stage whispered with a twinkling look at her husband.

"I did not say dull."

"I believe the word was 'repetitive.' And Eliza won't find them so, because she hasn't seen any."

"Very well," Westing grumbled, though he didn't actually look displeased. Maybe they all needed a distraction.

Phoebe grinned, showing she knew all along her husband would agree. Eliza smiled at their picture of marital happiness. Could it ever be the same for her? Unlikely if her father had his way.

After breakfast, the ladies dressed for a trip outside. Eliza spent several minutes at the mirror in her chamber, fighting with her curls. She reached out to the water on her dressing tables and summoned it to swirl, causing several drops to splash out and fly to her waiting fingers. She dabbed the last disobedient lock into place. All in order. Perfect.

Feeling shipshape and Bristol fashion, Eliza met Phoebe in the drawing room. Max came in still dusty from an early morning ride. His mood looked much improved.

"Dressed for an excursion?" he asked after a quick glance around the room.

"We're going to Lyme," Phoebe said. "You'll come with us, won't you? You haven't had a chance to see much of the town yet."

He looked a little cornered and shrugged one shoulder. "Suppose so."

Parry joined them, his boots polished to a high gloss, and his coat tailored to display his broad chest. Only a slight limp gave away the fact that one of his limbs was a false leg created by the renowned Mr. Cork. The eye patch was more conspicuous, but in a sailing town, he would probably be in good company. He made himself at home just as easily in a London ballroom, though. Eliza envied his ability to be comfortable anywhere. She rarely felt completely at ease, always wondering what others expected of her.

"And you must come to, I suppose?" Eliza asked him.

He grinned. "I would not let you out of my sight, especially not by the shore. What kind of trustee would I be if I allowed you to be swept out to sea?"

"Oh, really!" Eliza rolled her eyes.

"He's not entirely wrong," Westing said, striding into the room as he adjusted his cuff. "The sea wall is dangerous when there's a storm, and they are beaches that can be accessed as long as the tide is low, but when it comes back in, you might find yourself trapped there. It would be deadly."

"Certainly, you'll steer us away from any dangers," Eliza said.

Westing shrugged. "I don't mind having another helpful set of hands around for once."

"Beg your pardon!" Max exclaimed.

Westing gave him a wicked grin and went on, "But if we are to get back before dark, we must set out."

"You must point out the dragon tor to Captain Parry and Miss Prescott," Max said.

"Dragon tor?" Eliza asked, her curiosity piqued. Was that the rise she had seen from her window?

"A place that locals believe a great dragon is hibernating," Phoebe said.

"I can't confirm it's true," Westing said quickly. "There's no clear way into the mound as with some of those in Wales and the North, but the legend is an old one."

"The way the coast keeps sliding down in chunks," Phoebe said, "the dragon may be revealed one of these days."

"What do you think would happen then?" Eliza asked.

"Who knows?" Phoebe scratched Mushroom's head. "So little is known of older dragons. Perhaps it would just keep sleeping."

Eliza considered that as they fetched their gloves and went out to the carriage. Westing drove Phoebe and Eliza while Parry and Max rode alongside.

Phoebe pointed out the dragon tor when they passed. It was the same rise that Eliza had seen from her room, standing sentinel along the cliffs.

"Not much to see," Max said, keeping his horse alongside the carriage.

"Yes," Westing agreed. "One only knows about the legend because it has been passed down over time."

"Do they know what sort of dragon it's supposed to be?" Eliza asked.

Phoebe shook her head. "I've heard several guesses from our neighbors, but West tells me it's lost in the mists of time."

But Eliza noticed the behaviors of their own dragons as they rolled past. Amethyst perked her head up and gazed with interest at the tor, and the other two dragons stopped play fighting to look as well.

Eliza pointed it out to Phoebe.

"Perhaps there is a dragon there, then," Phoebe said, her eyes bright. "Few people have seen an adult dragon up close. It must be quite a sight."

Westing glanced up from the reins. "They are believed to be linked in some way to the land, bringing prosperity and so forth."

"Like the dragon under the Tower of London!" Max exclaimed. "If he ever leaves, England will fall."

"Certainly, the tower would fall," Eliza said, thinking of how large an animal would have to be to create the mound they were passing.

"Let's hope that the Dorset Dragon never awakens, then," Phoebe said. "I'm certain it would disrupt the estate!"

Eliza nodded. And if the luck of the land really was tied to its dragon's magic, it would be hard on everyone to lose a dragon. Fortunately, adult dragons rarely awakened. There were a few old stories, but certainly nothing in recent memory. Young dragons went off when their linked human died, and what happened to them after that only a few naturalists guessed at.

The road down to Lyme was steep, twisting through green hills, but they finally reached the town. The road looked like it would drop them right into the sea, but it turned just before it reached the beach. It was a pretty little village set against a small bay, with dark cliffs rising up on either side and a great stone wall curving out into the sea to protect it from the surges of capricious waves. Eliza felt more at ease seeing that. She sensed the great power of the sea and also its great indifference. It could smash away people, villages, probably even great sleeping dragons, and hardly note their passage any more than one would regard a tiny insect.

Westing drove them to the stable of the Royal Lion Inn, and from there it was an easy walk down cobbled streets to the seaside promenade and the sea wall—the Cobb, Westing called it. On the inside curve of the Cobb, there was a lower walkway that they followed past moored fishing boats, safe in the shelter of the wall. But the waves crashed against the far side of the wall, the ceaseless pounding of a force that would someday win and break all things before it.

Eliza hesitated when they reached stairs leading to the top of the Cobb, but she took Parry's hand and let him guide her up the rough stone steps. At the top of the wide sea wall, she stopped to stare out at the waters. In the distance, they were blue and green, but as they rolled closer to the bay, they took on a rusty orange. So different from the seas around Dominica, and yet, they were all connected.

"A lovely sight, is it not?" Parry asked, almost in her ear.

She gave a start and stared at him, and for a moment they just looked at each other, the wind brushing through their hair and whispering against their skin, and Eliza felt alone and oddly embarrassed in his company.

Then Phoebe called to them, and the moment was over. Parry offered his arm as they strolled the top of the Cobb, but it was like any other time that he escorted her, just fulfilling his duty to watch over her, no matter how ridiculous she thought his seriousness over the matter. He could only be doing it to tease her. Otherwise, he would certainly find some more amusing way to spend his time than squiring her around the countryside.

They followed the curve of the seawall until it met up again with the beach. The roar of the surf was like a pressure on Eliza, but as much as it pushed her away, it also seemed to draw her in. She shivered and leaned on Parry's sturdy arm.

They walked along the rocky shore westward to Monmouth Beach, and Phoebe excitedly pointed out the fossils embedded in the large black stones scattered over the beach.

Eliza broke away from Parry to examine them, and Amethyst bounded along the shore, tail high and nose to the ground. Most of the fossils appeared to be shells so old they had turned to stone, though some showed imprints of ancient plants or animals.

"Perhaps from the creation of the world," Phoebe exclaimed.

"Amazing!" Eliza plucked a small spiral fossil shell from the beach to keep.

She brushed off the damp, sticky sand to reveal the smooth, black surface. It felt like a sea pebble in her palm, but she could imagine that it was once the home of a creature. Sort of a way of living forever.

They all examined several gigantic stones embedded with many fossils—even Westing, who forgot that they were repetitive—and by the time the tide began to return and they made their way back up toward the seawall, they were exhausted and happy in their conversations and speculations about the past creatures who occupied the coast.

"I wonder if there were dragons back then," Phoebe said. "But then, there were no humans for them to bond with."

"The Bible tells us that God gave dragons to mankind to be

companions in a fallen world," Westing said. "I suppose that means our fates have always been intertwined."

Eliza smiled and patted Amethyst affectionately. She would be happy without the constant pressure of the sea, but she could not imagine being without Amethyst.

"There are the Assembly Rooms." Phoebe pointed to a pale blue building with many windows perched above a rocky point on the beach. "You'll love dancing there—it's like sailing above the waves."

"Probably too loud to hear the music above the surf," Parry said unromantically.

Eliza glowered at him.

"Come this way!" Phoebe called when they reached the street level again. She motioned them toward a little stone house near the shore on the east side of town. "We have to go to Mary Anning's. She didn't have her table set up by the inn, so this is the best place to buy more unusual fossils."

They climbed the steep steps and Phoebe knocked on the door. A young, dark-haired girl, perhaps twelve or thirteen, opened it.

"Have you come for fossils?" the girl asked, taking in the party.

"We have," Phoebe said. "Do you have any interesting ones today?"

Eliza and Parry exchanged a surprised look. This child was the premier fossil hunter?

The girl studied them then nodded. "I have some nice ones for you ladies and gents to look at."

The girl let them into the cottage. Worn curtains and much-repaired furniture had been carefully arranged in the parlour only to be crowded by low tables laden with various stones and fossils. It smelled of the beach, salty and slightly damp.

Amethyst sniffed around with interest, but Eliza called the dragon back before she could damage anything. Though Eliza had not planned to buy another fossil when she already found one on the beach, she immediately decided to make a purchase from the family, even if she had to wrestle the coin purse from Parry. That thought made her cheeks warm, so she quickly set it aside. What difficult circumstances would make a girl of twelve support her family by selling trinkets she had scrounged from the beach or dug from the cliffs?

But the trinkets Mary Anning displayed were enough to convince Eliza that her purchase would not be made out of charity. Mary had more lovely specimens of fossils than Eliza had seen on the beach, some with iridescent colors and in unusual shapes. She selected several fine pieces, thinking to have them made into jewelry. A part of land and ocean both, but solid and unthreatening.

Her selections were not cheap, and she turned to Parry, ready to demand he relinquish some of her funds, but there was no need. He already had the coin purse ready, his expression full of understanding. She smiled at him, once again in charity with her trustee, and counted out the coins for Mary.

"You have such marvelous fossils," Eliza said. "Do you find them yourself?"

Mary looked pleased and a little embarrassed. "Yes, miss. With my brother Joseph sometimes."

"How do you manage to discover such unique objects?"

Mary rubbed her arm and shrugged. "I have a knack for it, I guess. We go out when the storms have knocked some of the cliffside down so we can find the fossils before they're washed out to sea."

Dangerous, this girl's occupation. Eliza pointed to what looked like a piece of bone embedded in rock. "This one doesn't look like a shell."

"I think it's from an ancient creature, miss."

Eliza nodded, a little unnerved to think she was looking at the remnants of life long extinguished. But Phoebe lifted the bone and borrowed her husband's quizzing glass to study it, her eyes shining with wonder. She glanced at Westing, who rolled his eyes a little but nodded.

"I'll take this one," Phoebe said. "I need to come here more often to see what new things you have."

Mary looked thoughtful for a moment, then glanced at Phoebe and Westing's dragons and seemed to make up her mind about something. "Come back in a week or so, and I might have something you'll particularly like, if you're interested in ancient creatures."

"I will," Phoebe promised. She glanced at Westing. "Perhaps we should come for the assembly ball."

"If you like," he said, his voice pained.

Phoebe gave Eliza a warning glance. "No matter how much a man may seem to enjoy dancing when he is single, once he is married, it becomes a chore to him."

Westing raised her hand and kissed it. "Because now its main purpose is accomplished, and the pursuit can never afford the same pleasure as the reward."

Phoebe blushed, and Max rolled his eyes.

"Say," he said, his glance falling on another fossil. "This one is interesting. Almost looks like a giant tooth. I'll take it."

Mary gave a little start. "I hadn't meant to put that one out, but since you like it…"

Max happily paid the price Mary named. Eliza saw the girl's dilemma. She probably wanted many of the pieces herself, but she wanted food and a roof over her head more.

They took their new treasures and headed back to the Royal Lion for supper.

The private parlor was not available, so they ate in the common room with the scent of ale and fried fish strong around them. There was a great deal of talk about the dead men, and Eliza found it did not encourage her appetite. Westing frowned, Max's face was drawn in worry, and Parry ate nothing at all. Their party was quiet enough to hear the other conversations.

"No one knows who the other man was," someone said. "Billy George should not have gotten mixed up with a stranger."

"He was talking crazy lately. Someone was putting wild ideas in his head. Saying things about—" The man hesitated and looked over at the party of gentry. "Well, things that don't concern him."

Parry's eyebrows went up at that. Eliza glanced at Westing, but his face remained impassive. Still, she thought he had heard, too. Whatever these men wanted to keep from Westing, he would probably be obliged to dig into. Brainy Jamie was no doubt useful for that. Eliza didn't want to think about those poor dead men, but she certainly didn't want their killers to go unpunished, either.

The conversation they overheard had cast a temporary pall over their group, but by the time they rode home, the sun setting over the green fields and the sky delicious shades of orange and peach-pink, they were once again in a tired but cheerful mood, examining their new treasures and speaking about the sea.

They rode past the dragon tor without anyone commenting on it, but Eliza noticed how her dragon perked up once again as they passed it. She scratched Amethyst's ear ridges and gazed at the tor as well, imagining the dragon sleeping beneath it and wondering what her own dragon sensed about the ancient creature. Did it sleep forever, slowly melding into the ground it protected, or was it aware on some level of the small people and small dragons passing by? She shivered and pulled her cloak around her, thinking, for once, that it might be better to go unnoticed.

Chapter Five

THE TROUBLE WASN'T OVER, Parry knew. Much as they might want to leave the justice of the peace to sort out the dead men in the boat, the reaction of the townspeople to Westing warned Parry that the mystery would follow their party until it was resolved. And trouble had a way of spreading if not ripped out early, like how a bit of rot on the hull of a ship would foul the wood around it, too, until the whole thing sunk.

Westing would never let his ship sink, and Parry liked Westing well enough to want to help the man. Besides, a wrong had been done against a fellow man of the sea. It felt like a personal affront.

The morning after their excursion into town, he walked out to the cliff above where they had found the boat. It was a nasty piece of shoreline—one of those places where a person could get caught at high tide with nowhere to go and get beaten against the rocks by the rising waves.

It was the same beach where he had watched Eliza stroll barefoot, her eyes shining at something Lady Westing said and the sun reflecting off her glossy black curls. A sparkling moment. But it was gone, as thoroughly erased as the soft footprints she had left in the sand.

The tide was low now, and Parry spotted a figure walking along the beach. He squinted at the water, trying to determine if the tide was rising, but it appeared to be at low ebb. Hopefully, that meant the person below knew what he was doing.

Curious, Parry snuck down the path to get a better look. In theory, the figure was trespassing on Westing's land, though Parry didn't think the viscount was very protective of his coasts. More of his income came from rents than fishing. But this person could have some connection to the dead men.

Parry found a safe outcrop of rocks and wedged his way into it. A sharp rock pressed into his back, but he made himself as comfortable as possible. It was one of those times that missing a leg was an advantage—let him squeeze in a little tighter. Climbing back out would be a trick, but he'd worry about that when the time came. Just as it had at sea, his luck always seemed to get him through.

From his perch, he could see the figure clearly. It was not a "he" but a "she." The girl Mary Anning they had bought the fossils from. He grinned to himself. Was the naughty lass taking fossils from Westing's land only to sell them back to him? His smile faded. Was that the kind of thing a respectable man reported to his host? Probably. Parry hated trying to be respectable. It fit him like a poorly tailored coat. He could pride himself on always doing what his honor demanded, and at sea that had been enough. But his life as a captain was over, and now he wasn't certain what he was supposed to be. He was no scoundrel, but he wasn't quite a gentleman, either. His parents were well-born— country gentry—but they had been happy to dump young Parry on the navy, as he was a bit too rambunctious for home. And where did that leave him now? Adrift.

Parry watched Mary Anning's careful progress across the beach. She worked hard to help her family. And Westing wouldn't begrudge a child the chance to put food in her mouth. No, Parry wouldn't be one to tattle on the girl. Perhaps, though, he could hint to Eliza that she could fossil hunt closer to the estate. Eliza liked to shop, but she might like finding her own fossils as well.

The thought distracted him for a moment, but then he turned his attention back to the girl. She was bold, not only to be trespassing, but also to be doing so alone. She must have had a sibling or friend who could come with her for protection. Hadn't she mentioned a brother?

The thought of a young girl alone on the shore worried Parry enough that he went into his most watchful mode, studying the horizon line of the ocean to be sure no one was about. Of course, alone wasn't dangerous. It was alone with someone else that could put a person in peril.

Something whooshed overhead, and Parry ducked, twisting to see around the blind spot from his ruined eye. He hated the disadvantage that gave him in a fight.

But this wasn't a projectile from an assailant. A cat-sized dragon swooped down to the beach. His eyebrows went up. He usually didn't see dragons flying that high. Didn't think they quite had their wings figured out yet. This one, he realized, was actually only gliding. It floated down to the beach, then hopped and scrambled up the cliffside to sail on the breezes. Clever creature.

And he looked at the girl, the only person around. Was the dragon hers? But she lived in such poverty. Being chosen as a dragon's companion opened up all the possibilities of the *haut ton*, since the upper ranks of Society wanted to both use and monitor the magic dragons bestowed on their humans.

There were a few dragon-linked who chose to avoid Society for one reason or another. The threat of the anti-magic Luddites was one issue. And though Parry wanted to establish a respectable place for himself in the world, he understood the yearning for freedom. As the sea breeze sang past his ears and he watched the dragon and the girl going happily about their business, he could relate to a desire to never give that up for the strictures of Society. Not even his missing eye and leg had turned Parry completely from the sea. His guardianship of Eliza had tied him to London, but he carried a thin hope, as faint as a mermaid's song, that he might remedy that someday, as well.

Mary had collected a basket of fossils and now made her way back along the beach, glancing occasionally at the waves to be sure they did not creep too close. Parry nodded. Good girl. She was a child of the shore and knew to watch the tides. The dragon followed along, confirming his suspicion that it was linked to the child.

Once she was safe, out of his sight and hopefully where she would not be prey to tides or men, Parry straightened and climbed from his hiding place. He contemplated the mystery of Mary Anning as he walked. Did the town know of her dragon? Sometimes, town folk were not friendly to the dragon-linked among them, being superstitious about their abilities. They tolerated it among the nobility because they had little choice—except those Luddites and Levelers who would overthrow every dragon-linked person—but they looked askance on one of their own who seemed out of place with their dragon. The girl might keep it a secret from all.

Parry strolled back toward the house. He was surprised to see Eliza walking the garden path. She hadn't seen him yet, and the sun played off her black curls, shining like the light on the waves. She was staring at the dragon tor.

He glanced in the direction of the tor. Not being dragon-linked himself, he wasn't sure what to think about the rumors that dragons slumbered all over the land, keeping it alive in some mysterious way. But he didn't have any objections to the rumors. He had seen enough strange things at sea—lights and fires on the horizon, the crests of great monsters that had no name—that he could easily accept other things he didn't understand.

"Do you sense anything from it?" he asked Eliza without preamble when he got close.

She started and gave him an exasperated look that made her eyes glitter. But then she grew serious.

"You know, perhaps I do. I think Amethyst does for certain. I wonder if the creature is awake and sort of trapped under there, or if it's just slumbering for all this time."

"I can imagine it sleeping," Parry said. "Like an old sailor. This is the dragon's retirement."

"I do like that thought better than it being trapped. I suppose we can't know."

"They say the Red Dragon of Wales is sleeping under its hill. Supposedly, some shepherds have stumbled across it or heard its snores. And it sounds like they were anxious to keep it that way." He gestured to Amethyst. "These little fellows aren't very threatening, but a much larger cousin would be a terror."

Amethyst hissed at him, and he laughed. Eliza smiled and scratched her dragon's scales.

"Don't worry, dear," she said. "You are perfectly ferocious."

"Yes, pardon me for misspeaking," Parry said, trying not to laugh at the offended little creature. It impressed him how much they seemed to understand.

"Coming back for dinner?" Parry asked, offering an arm.

He was certain she would refuse him just to be contrary, but after a moment and another glance back at the tor, she nodded and took his arm. Her hand was warm and light where it rested on his sleeve. They strolled back to the house in companionable silence, just them and the sea wind at their backs. It felt comfortable, but Parry knew it could not last. Even his luck wasn't that good.

Chapter Six

THERE WERE TIMES, Eliza thought, that Captain Parry was quite tolerable. He often made her smile in spite of herself, and there was something reassuring about his presence, and sometimes, though she would never admit it to him, about his common-sense conversation as well. Like an anchor.

He made it almost to the end of supper the next day before he fell out of her good graces again.

"I hope you managed to amuse yourself today without any shops to visit," he teased as he dished some roast pigeon onto her plate.

She raised an eyebrow. "I'm quite capable of keeping myself occupied, thank you."

"I can see that. It's a fetching new hairstyle you've concocted."

She eyed him warily. The damp sea air made her hair difficult to tame, and she'd spent several hours finding the best way to arrange her curls, but now she wasn't sure if Parry really liked it or if he was quizzing her.

"I suppose if even a sailor can appreciate it, then it was time well spent," she said stiffly.

"No, seems like a waste to me," he said, taking a bite of stewed apple.

"A waste!"

Amethyst growled at Parry, but he offered her a piece of chicken from his plate. Amethyst gobbled it up—the little traitor—and settled in to watch him expectantly, her tail curled around her legs. Meanwhile, Parry studied Eliza's hair like he was evaluating the seaworthiness of a new vessel.

"Is it sailors you're trying to impress now?" he asked. "I doubt anyone you meet here will notice the effort you put into it, much less appreciate it."

"Many fashionable people enjoy Lyme in the autumn," Eliza snapped. She was counting on it, in fact. She had to find her dandy to alarm her father out of his controlling ways.

"That is true," Phoebe said, jumping in before their shots off the bow became a real fray. "We may meet any number of the *ton* here during Lyme's little season."

Parry frowned at that. "Still seems wasteful. You care so much for them, but what do they care for you?"

Eliza felt cold at his words. Perhaps Parry couldn't be expected to know she was nervous about her first social appearance in Lyme Regis, but he didn't have to be so flippant about it. In London, she was accepted because she had a dragon and respectable wealth, though she feared without those she might just be seen as an upstart. How would it be in Lyme Regis? Her West Indies origins might not find as much acceptance there.

Phoebe jumped in with a change in topic, but Captain Parry's comments left Eliza in a sour mood.

The arrival of Mr. Blanding, the justice of the peace, cast a pall over the whole party. Westing agreed to gather everyone in the dining room to speak with him. The man cast nervous glances around at the three dragons in the room: Mushroom curled on Phoebe's lap, Amethyst hopping onto the sideboard to get a higher perch, and Dragon circling the uneasy magistrate.

"How can we help you?" Westing said, his voice a little chilly, and a quizzing glass dangling from his fingers, ready to be wielded against the man if he proved impertinent.

Eliza found herself glad that she did not have to face him in his lord of the manor role.

Blanding licked his lips nervously. "It's just something I've come across in asking questions about those poor lads who were killed."

Westing raised an eyebrow, signaling for him to go on.

The man cleared his throat. "You see, my lord, there's talk that Billy George, the local boy, was running his mouth about something that had to do with dragons." Here he fumbled to a stop and flushed bright red. "Not that I would ever question—"

"Us?" Westing held up the quizzing glass, studying the candlelight reflecting off of it.

The magistrate's eyes widened enough to show that the thought had crossed his mind and he was now chasing it away like a blackbird from a grain field. "No, I would never presume! Not me."

Westing sighed and let the quizzing glass fall. "You should question us, though. I won't have it said that I don't want justice done."

"Of course not. I only wondered… the only dragons in the area… perhaps there was some threat to you?"

It was almost imperceptible, but Westing's face turned a shade paler, and Phoebe gave a start at the man's words.

"Are you aware of any Luddite activities in the area?" Westing asked.

"Not here, sir," the magistrate said quickly, apparently glad to be able to deliver this news. "But I thought you should be on your guard, in case…"

Westing eyed him. "In case. Yes, thank you for keeping us apprised."

The butler showed the man out, but the door had hardly closed behind him before Phoebe sank back on the sofa.

"It's Shaw!" Her fingers trembled and she clenched them together. Sparks of light flashed and faded above her head. "He's come for us."

"Now, dear." Westing sat beside her and placed a hand over hers. "We don't have any reason to suspect that. They might not have had anything at all to do with us and our dragons. I've had Jamie ask around, and he says Billy George was getting a reputation for asking a great many prying questions."

"Like a spy?" Parry asked.

"Perhaps. At least, someone who was involved in something dangerous. But it must be something local. How would a local lad get involved with the likes of Shaw?"

"That's right," Max said, perhaps a little too assuredly. "That villain would have no reason to be here. We're safe. Must be."

Phoebe nodded at this reassurance, and the sparks overhead flickered out, but Eliza's stomach tightened. They'd heard nothing of Shaw for some time, but he was the leader of the anti-magic Luddites determined to drive out dragons from England as they were doing in France with their Reign of Terror. Shaw even managed to avoid the snares of the slippery Lord Blackerby. He could be doing anything.

"Anyone want to play cards?" Max suggested.

Everyone mumbled assent to his plan, but it was a quiet, strained group that shuffled, dealt, and placed imaginary bets on their hands.

They were safe, though, Eliza told herself. Westing's small army of servants would not let just anyone come striding into the house. And dragons would fight to defend themselves and their linked human. An angry dragon could be fearsome, despite their small size. Shaw, though, knew a great deal about dragons, including how to poison them. No one, as far as Eliza knew, could kill a dragon, but Shaw could make them ill, which also made their human ill. Westing would probably have their food stores watched carefully.

It was also possible, as Westing had said, that the dragons the man had been asking about had nothing to do with them. That should have reassured Eliza, since it meant she was safe, but it worried her even more if there was some plot brewing just beneath the peaceful veneer of the countryside.

The party broke up early, happy to retreat to the safety of bolted bedroom doors. Eliza couldn't sleep, though. She thought she had escaped the Luddites by leaving London, but now it felt as though they were following her. More likely following Westing and Phoebe, since they were the ones who had tangled with Shaw in the past. Eliza threw off her blanket and slipped out of the bed curtains. She pulled on a dressing gown and walked to her window to sit heavily, resting her elbows on the chilly plastered sill. She didn't look for trouble, and she just wanted it to leave her alone.

But something nagged at her. A call from the darkness.

Danger. Danger. Danger.

She stood and glared out toward the sea. Why could it not leave her in peace?

Something moved below in the gardens. It could be an animal. Or a person who had every reason to be sneaking about at night. In the darkness. Without so much as a lantern.

Eliza drew a deep breath and leaned forward, trying to see better. Yes, there was definitely a figure there, in the deepest darkness. Someone adept at moving in shadows. Perhaps a thief or a murderer. She clutched her dressing gown and rushed out into the hall. Captain Parry's door was closest to hers. She pounded.

"Captain Parry! Someone is sneaking in the gardens outside!"

He was at the door in an instant, still alert and fully dressed. "Where?"

"Right below my window."

Parry nodded and stormed down the stairs. Westing, probably roused by the noise, dashed out of his room in his dressing gown, following Parry without stopping to ask what the trouble was. Dragon bounded along with him, leaving a trail of frost where his claws touched the wood floor.

Phoebe, looking half asleep, nearly stumbled into Eliza. "What's happening?"

"I saw someone outside my window, sneaking in the dark."

Phoebe's eyes cleared. "Let's go see."

They ran to Eliza's window, and Phoebe sent a glowing orb outside just in time to catch the men trying to study the ground with a lantern. They glanced up briefly then resumed their search. After a quarter of an hour, Phoebe's light began to dim, and the men circled back for the house. The two ladies hurried out to meet them at the top of the stairs.

"Did you find anything?" Phoebe asked.

Westing shook his head. "But I made sure the doors are secured, and the servants have been put on guard. It might have just been someone passing through. Or shadows playing tricks..."

He didn't sound convinced. Or convincing.

Westing guided Phoebe back to their room. Eliza looked to Parry.

"I know I saw something. It wasn't just a trick of the shadows."

He sighed. "I know, love. I saw the footprints. Westing knows it, too. But whoever it is, they're gone now."

Eliza nodded and went back to her room, sliding the bolt. That made her feel a little safer, but perhaps not as much as knowing that Parry was just a few rooms away and would answer so quickly when she called.

Chapter Seven

PARRY AWOKE the next morning still troubled by the events of the night before. It was his job to keep Eliza safe, and he was doing a terrible job so far. Men with their throats cut, shadows sneaking about the estate at night. He wanted to believe it had nothing to do with them or their dragons, and especially that it had nothing to do with the revolutionary Shaw, but his gut said otherwise. It had always warned him when a storm was coming at sea, and he could practically smell the sharp hurricane winds now.

Max was the only one who came to breakfast looking chipper. He hummed a dance tune to himself and picked up a hard roll from the side board, juggling it from hand to hand. He stopped when he caught sight of the weary, somber faces around the table.

"Bad news?" he asked.

"I can't believe you slept through it!" Phoebe said. "Someone was sneaking around the garden last night."

Max dropped the roll, which bounced on the table, and sat next to his sister. "What? Sneaking about here? Did you get a good look at him?"

Westing shook his head. "We tried to catch him, but he disappeared."

Max toyed with his knife, his brow knit with worry. Parry watched him closely. His instincts told him the young man knew or suspected something that he wasn't sharing.

Then Max put on a forced smile for his sister. "Is this place haunted, then?"

Phoebe chuckled weakly, and Westing rolled his eyes at Max. "It's not old enough. Though the more ancient family pile that descended through female lines to Lady Sophie has several rumored apparitions."

"Besides," Parry put in, "ghosts don't leave footprints."

Everyone grew quiet at that.

"Do you suppose we should miss the assembly ball?" Phoebe asked.

Westing jabbed at a slice of ham. "I won't be bullied on my own property. And we don't know that there is actually a threat against us personally. It could have been a smuggler or a potential housebreaker last night."

"If there is a threat," Parry added, "We're more likely to find it ourselves by prying around than waiting for the constables to dig it up."

That drew another shroud of worried quiet over the party. Phoebe stroked her dragon's back, her eyes wide and focused on some unpleasant memory. Eliza gave Parry a suspicious look. Well, she was correct. He was going to do some of his own prying around.

He started after breakfast by examining the footsteps in the garden by daylight. Multiple sets of footprints, in fact. He smelled a storm rolling in, and he needed to see what there was to see before the rain washed it away.

The gardener's prints were easy to identify by the hand wagon tracks that followed them. Parry's own steps were even more obvious by the limp from his false leg, and Westing's traced a similar path. That left two men's tracks that seemed suspicious.

The first were the ones they had spotted last night where Eliza had seen the stranger: long, thin boot prints with a confident stride. They knew the person who left them had been lurking about in the middle of the night because Eliza had spotted him, but he had not been hesitant about it. A local, perhaps? Or someone who had been in the area before.

The second odd footprints belonged to someone who had been trying to sneak, and had done so rather obviously. Not an expert thief. The marks of the boots showed someone who had sometimes stood still for long periods and sometimes turned back or circled around uncertainly. This was a stranger or else someone who was very hesitant about his course.

Parry wondered if the two sets met up, but as he tracked them, he found that the confident person had seemingly gone out of their way to avoid the path of the hesitant one. That made Parry more curious and concerned about both of them.

He circled back to the house to find Westing watching him with amusement.

"I think you've done my morning's work for me," Westing said, scanning the garden with his quizzing glass. "What did you find?"

Parry quickly explained the two sets of footprints.

"Hmm." Westing let his quizzing glass dangle. "Perhaps two men with very different objectives?"

"Or the same objective, but not working in tandem."

Westing sighed. "We are in a tangle, aren't we?"

"It seems that way." Parry grinned. "And to think, I worried the country might be dull."

Westing scoffed. "I have a sense you would find a way to make it interesting if it wasn't. I will have my footmen stay on the alert."

Parry nodded. He would be watching out his window at night, but with the weather changing, he wasn't likely to see much. And in town, he would pay close attention to anyone whose actions matched what he guessed from the boot prints, but that was a slim chance as well. His luck had its limits.

They set off for Lyme early the on day of the assembly so the ladies had time to pick up fresh trinkets. And so that Westing had more time to set Brainy Jamie to sneaking. Max protested that he couldn't bear to look at one more shop and would rather stay in and read. Phoebe looked unhappy about this, but she didn't argue with her brother.

Joshua, Westing's younger brother, ran out to gawk at the phaeton when the grooms brought it out.

"I want to go to town, too!" Joshua said.

"We're going to a ball," Phoebe said. "You would not like to dance."

Joshua puffed out his chest. "I would if it were with you or Miss Prescott."

"I fear you would quickly grow bored," Westing said.

Brainy Jamie hopped into the rear seat of the phaeton, wearing a smirk. Joshua's mouth dropped open in indignation, and he gestured to the other boy.

"*He's* going with you, though?" Joshua demanded.

Westing looked uncomfortable. "He's going to help me with some business in Lyme."

"Business!" Joshua snorted. "I can spy, too. Give me the chance, and I could! I wager you wouldn't leave me behind if I had a dragon."

He looked so offended and betrayed, it tugged at Parry's heart. Westing exchanged an uneasy glance with Phoebe. Naturally, they couldn't tell the boy he would only be in Jamie's way.

"Of course, you could spy," Eliza said quickly. "But everyone in Lyme knows who you are. You would not want to give Lord Westing away. If you stay here, you can guard the house."

Joshua frowned at that, but Parry could see she had won the point. Clever lass, preserving the boy's sense of pride.

"Very well, I will stay," Joshua said, affecting a look so haughty, he could only have learned it from his brother.

Brainy Jamie stuck a tongue out at him and settled in for the ride with a grin. When Westing wasn't looking, Joshua stuck his tongue out in return. Parry smiled and pretended not to see.

Instead, he used the mounting block to swing up onto the horse Westing loaned him. The animal shifted uneasily beneath him. Parry appreciated that riding took the weight off his leg stump, but he was more at home on a ship or moving under his own power, and the animals always sensed it. Nevertheless, he brought the horse around and kept close to the carriage, scanning the surrounding woods for signs of trouble.

When they passed the dragon tor, Eliza's attention fixed on it, and Parry followed her gaze. He wondered, as he often did, what dragon magic felt like. He imagined it to be a bit like the sense he sometimes had for the way the wind and waves moved at sea—nothing definable, but a knowing he couldn't explain. To him, the tor was just another heap of dirt and rocks, but he guessed by the way Eliza stared at it that it had some pull on her. It made him uneasy, and he was glad enough to descend down to Lyme Regis and see the waves rolling into shore behind the sturdy stone and timber building.

They left the women and Jamie in front of the Royal Lion and turned their horses over to the ostler.

"The Three Cups is crowded with visitors from Bath," Westing said, explaining why he shunned the inn across the street with its semi-circle of large, inviting windows looking over the traffic below.

The Royal Lion was busy as well. Parry noted a high-spirited chestnut mare in the care of a long-faced groom. The horse looked familiar. He wasn't sure where he'd seen it, but it gave him an uneasy feeling. Someone from London—someone he didn't care for—was there in Lyme Regis. It could only add to their troubles.

Once they'd seen the horses cared for, Parry and Westing found the ladies admiring the goods in the shop windows. Westing took Phoebe's arm, but Parry knew Eliza wouldn't appreciate any such escort from him. He followed behind, enjoying the fresh, salty scent of the air.

Eliza stopped to decide between two pairs of gloves which looked identical to Parry. He hated to see Eliza wasting her time trying to impress people he doubted she really even liked, but she hadn't spent all of her pin money, so he couldn't do much to object.

Amethyst hopped down from Eliza's shoulder to help her inspect the gloves. It sniffed both pairs, then rubbed its head against one.

"The pair with the pearl buttons? You just want them for your hoard when they wear out, don't you?" Eliza asked, scratching the dragon's back.

The shopkeeper looked hopeful, so Parry guessed that the pearl buttons were more expensive.

But Eliza smiled at her dragon. "Very well. We'll take these."

"I need to see if the book shop has the newest Miss Charity novel," Phoebe said once Eliza had paid for her gloves.

Parry saw Eliza's lips tighten at the mention of Miss Charity. The author's thinly veiled portrayal of Eliza featured her as vain and silly. Parry understood why Eliza might seem that way to someone only seeing the surface, but it was an unfair assessment, missing Eliza's mind and heart, which were some of her better features. Along with the way her eyes sparkled like the sea when she laughed. But Parry couldn't convince Eliza to give up the fashionable books, even if they bothered her. At least he didn't feature in them. He didn't rank high enough in society, apparently, to be made a caricature.

"We need to go to the Anning house," Eliza said. "Remember, Miss Anning had something interesting to show us."

The men agreed, and they walked down the main road to the Anning's cottage. Parry grinned to himself, thinking of the girl finding fossils on Westing's land.

Eliza glanced at him and raised an eyebrow. "Why are you so particularly cheerful about shopping for fossils?"

His grin widened. "I admire Miss Anning's pluck."

That was no answer, and he could tell Eliza knew it, but she didn't pursue it. She understood by now Parry would not divulge a secret he was determined to keep.

When they got to the house, it seemed strangely quiet. Eliza climbed the stone steps and knocked. After a long delay, an older woman answered the door. It was so different from their first visit that Parry almost questioned if they had the right house.

The woman took in the assemblage of quality gathered on her doorstep and bobbed a dull curtsey.

"We are here to see Miss Anning," Eliza said, when the woman didn't seem to have anything to say to them.

"Mary—" the woman croaked.

"Yes, Mary Anning. She had something to show us. A new fossil, perhaps."

The woman began crying. Not a burst of sobs, but a slow trickle of weary tears down her lined cheeks. "I can't help you. My poor Mary. I don't know what to do."

Chapter Eight

A SWELL of hot sickness washed over Parry at the sight of Mrs. Anning's grief.

"What's the matter?" Phoebe asked, quickly stepping forward to take Mrs. Anning's hand. "Has something happened to Mary?"

The old woman looked at her, a little dazed. "I don't know. She went out two nights ago, and I haven't seen her since."

Parry maneuvered to the front. "Do you know where she went?"

"No, sir," the woman said in her low, creaking voice. "After some fossils. I always thought she was safe because she had—" the woman stopped, but the tears came faster.

"She had her dragon with her," Parry said.

Eliza's surprised gaze jumped to Parry, but the woman nodded, looking defeated. "She did."

"She's dragon-linked?" Phoebe asked.

"How do you know?" Westing said at the same time.

"I'll explain later." Parry turned back to Mrs. Anning. "And you have not seen either of them?"

The woman shook her head.

Parry looked to the rest of them. "Think, quickly. When a dragon owner dies, does the dragon fly off immediately, or does it return home?"

Phoebe's eyes widened at his bluntness, but Westing spoke up.

"It will usually stay near its linked person until they are buried, but it could return home to mourn before departing."

Parry looked to the woman, who did not seem to follow all of this conversation. "Mrs. Anning, we can hope your daughter is still alive, but we must search for her. She could be stranded somewhere."

Mrs. Anning reached out to him. "Thank you, sir. My son and I looked, but it's been stormy and dangerous, and I couldn't bear to lose him, too... I mean, in case..."

Parry squeezed her hand then turned back to the others. "We need to search along the shoreline. I'm going to find someone who can take me out in a boat to the places where the tide may have cut the girl off."

"I want to help, too," Eliza said, her expression defiant.

"Of course." Parry glanced at Westing. "You know the area best. Where should we spend our energy searching?"

"There are dangerous cliffs and beaches in both directions."

"This girl was local," Parry reminded him. "She knew the hazardous spots."

Phoebe's eyes widened. "Landslides!"

Westing's brow furrowed, and he nodded. "That's a good thought. Landslides aren't uncommon around here, and one may have cut the girl off when she normally would be able to get back."

Parry nodded. "I'll ask the fishermen about recent landslides. Are your dragons able to hunt for another dragon?"

The dragon-linked all looked at each other, and Westing sighed. "It's clear they understand some of what we say, but they don't exactly take orders."

"But sometimes they do take notice of other dragons," Eliza said. "We might watch their behavior for clues."

Parry nodded. "Very well. I'm going out in the boat. Westing, if you want to go west, then Lady Westing and Miss Prescott can go east."

Eliza looked like she was going to argue just for the sake of arguing, but she didn't. Perhaps it was the seriousness of the situation, or the fact that his arrangement kept the search respectable and safe for everyone. So, she only followed Phoebe down toward the beach.

Parry hurried to the Cobb, as near to a jog as he could come with his false leg. The stump would be sore the next day, but he would worry about that later. There was a child to find.

Several fishermen lounged about the lower stone walkway of the Cobb, working on nets. Parry approached an older man with gnarled hands. The man had the look of a real seaman about him.

"I need someone to take me out to sea," Parry said.

The man didn't even look up from the nets he was mending. "I don't give tours."

"I'm no tourist." Parry stepped closer, his wooden leg thumping unevenly on the stone of the Cobb.

The fisherman looked up, his frown softening as he took in Parry's commanding look. "A sailor, are you? Lost your leg to the Monster in France?"

"In the West Indies."

The old man nodded. "I have a son in the blockade." He squinted against the bright light reflecting off the waves. "My hands are too tired to do more rowing today, but I have another boy who can take you out."

Parry nodded his thanks. "I'll pay you handsomely."

"I wouldn't say no to that. Thank you, sir."

The boy was a teenaged lad who looked bored with the idea of rowing Parry out along the shoreline, but he shrugged and did as his father asked.

Before they set off, Parry looked back to the old fisherman. "Are you aware of any landslides in the last two days?"

Father and son exchanged glances. The father started to shake his head but stopped. "Oh, aye! I do recall seeing one." He looked to his son. "By the big rocks to the east, just before Charmouth."

The boy nodded, and they set off in the boat. Parry pulled out a spyglass—much more practical than the quizzing glasses favored by dandies of London—and scanned the shore with his good eye. He spotted Lady Westing and Eliza trekking along the beach, and his gaze lingered for a moment on Eliza. Staying out of trouble. Then he scanned onward.

They rowed along, the waves rocking them soothingly and the sun beating off the water to warm the salt-scented spray. Parry was careful not to let the peacefulness of the scene lull him. Soon, they lad pointed out the recent landslide.

"How close can you get us?" Parry asked.

"Right close to the shore, if you like."

"I do like."

They rowed along near the shore, Parry still using his scope. The landslide was a raw and brutal gash in the cliffs, still fresh. Many large rocks littered the shore and had tumbled down to the water's edge. If a dragon had been caught with its human, how long would it take the creature to burrow free? The dragon would survive while the human did not, and no one would know for some time. Parry felt a sinking dread as he scanned the rocks, motionless except for the occasional flutter of seabirds.

Movement caught his eye. "Wait, there!"

The lad looked up at him. "Sir?"

"I think I see someone next to the landslide." Parry kept the spyglass trained on the landslide. "Can you land here?"

"I don't know. It's rocky."

"Never mind. Row as close as you can, and I'll swim over. I need you to head back and find two ladies walking along the shore in this direction. Tell them Captain Parry said to hurry this way."

The young man nodded and maneuvered the boat closer to the beach. Parry stripped off his jacket, boots, and wooden leg and tied them into a sling around his shoulders. He slid out of the boat into the cold waters. The icy waves gave him a momentary shock, then he struck out for the shore. The water quickly turned shallow and rocky, so he half-swam, half-stumbled his way to the shore.

Parry pulled himself up against a rock, his leg still in the sling of his jacket. He hopped a few steps and called, "Miss Anning?"

"Is someone there?" a weak voice said.

Parry's luck was holding. He strapped on his leg and hobbled forward, scanning the landslide. Mary leaned against the warm side of a boulder. And standing guard above her was a small, red dragon.

Parry climbed closer. The dragon flapped its wings in agitation, and the girl seemed to pull into herself more tightly.

"You're Miss Anning, aren't you?" he asked, stopping his approach. "I met you a sennight ago. You showed me and my friends some fossils."

She tilted her head, still her expression wary and confused. Dehydration, he realized. It hadn't rained for several days, and she had nothing but the salty foam of the channel to tease her with the promise of water without actually slacking her thirst. He had seen it drive men mad, and she was just a mite.

"My friends are coming this way, too," he said. "The ones with the dragons. We'll help you get out. Are you trapped?"

She nodded at this, seeming to rouse herself a little. "How will your friends get here?" she asked in a raspy voice that barely sounded above the waves.

He studied the landslide. It was a nasty one, unstable looking and full of boulders. A young girl would have trouble climbing it. Come to think of it, so would a sailor with only one leg. Westing or Max Hart could hop over it like a pair of seals, but two ladies in gowns?

"They can climb. Or they might take a boat like I did. Only, the boat couldn't get to the beach here, so we will have to do a little walking. Do you think you can stand?"

She mumbled something, and Parry limped closer, stumbling a bit over the rock-strewn shore. The girl's leg was at an odd angle. Her dragon extended its long neck and flapped its wings in annoyance at Parry.

"I fell trying to climb," she said quietly.

"I see. May I look? I will be very careful not to hurt you." He pointed to his own leg and grinned. "This one used to bother me, but it doesn't anymore."

She chuckled weakly at his poor joke—a good sign. She made no objection when he lowered himself to the ground next to her and poked a little at the injury. She didn't flinch, but she did wiggle a bit, so she had feeling. A good sign. The bone wasn't protruding and the bruising wasn't severe, so he thought she would recover.

He shook his head. "Bad news, my girl."

She looked at him with wide eyes.

"I'm afraid you're not going to get a fine wooden leg like mine. This looks like it will heal up just fine once we get you home to your mother."

She laughed more sincerely this time—more, he knew, from relief than from his sad attempts at humor.

"I don't think I can carry you over that mudslide, and I did not have the foresight to bring anything for you to drink, but I will keep you safe until my friends get here. You know, we came to your house because you had said you had something interesting to show us. Is that what you were after when this happened?"

She nodded, looking reluctant to speak. He wouldn't press her there. Instead, he distracted her by asking about some of the shells and fossils obvious there on the beach after the fresh landslide.

"Captain Parry?" Phoebe's voice drifted to them over the landslide.

"Yes, here! I have Miss Anning, but she'll need some help getting over the rocks. Careful! It's unstable."

There were a few moments of nothing but the sound of waves and seabirds calling, and then Phoebe's head popped over the top of the rocks.

"Oh, dear," Phoebe said.

Eliza appeared beside her; concern etched on her face.

"Miss Anning," Parry said. "Do you remember Lady Westing and Miss Prescott? They can help you off of this pile of rocks and then fuss over you. They might not have anything to drink, but I would not be surprised if one of them had a sweet in her reticule. You can be brave, can't you?"

Miss Anning nodded.

Eliza had a distracted, thoughtful expression, like she was listening to something far away. "I think I can get her a little fresh water."

She scrambled farther up the rock slide and, after pausing with her head tilted, made a lifting gesture. A trickle of water drifted up from the rocks like a waterfall in reverse. Eliza drew a circling motion with her finger, and the water spun into a water spout, which obediently followed her back to where Mary waited.

"This will be a touch messy," Eliza warned.

Mary nodded and opened her mouth. Eliza gestured the tiny water spout closer so Mary could sip from it until it fell apart with a splash.

"Thank you," Mary said hoarsely.

Eliza and Phoebe supported the girl between them and picked their way across the rocky landslide. Parry followed even more slowly, the straps of his wooden leg rubbing salt into his skin. If he could clean up at the inn, he might not be in too much pain the next day. He was grateful to be able to walk, but he wished it didn't come at such a cost. In the meantime, however, he kept a stoic face. The captain doesn't show fear or pain.

On the other side, he found Phoebe worrying over Miss Anning's ankle, while Eliza studied the cliffs with a deep frown.

"What is troubling you, my sweet?" Parry asked.

She didn't even bother rolling her eyes at him, a sign of how deeply she was troubled by what she saw.

"I'm not entirely certain," she said. "But something feels wrong about this to me."

Parry turned to look up at the cliffs. "Westing warned us that landslides are common along here."

"Perhaps," she said. "Where the cliff is overhanging the sea and collapses. But look how the cliff broke away here, like a chunk of it was gouged out."

Parry raised an eyebrow. "You think this was deliberate?"

"I don't know." She lowered her voice. "But I think we should mention it to Westing."

Parry nodded, casting a worried look at the cliffs above.

Chapter Nine

ONCE MISS ANNING was safely installed at home, a physician attending to her leg, and her mother tearfully hovering nearby, Eliza drew Westing aside to tell him about the landslide.

He frowned as she described what she saw. "Yes, it does sound odd."

"Could it have been done deliberately?" Phoebe asked. "To harm the girl?"

"I'm not sure why," Westing said, "but it bears considering. Do you know what her dragon is attuned to?"

Eliza shook her head.

"I've been speaking to the girls' mother," Phoebe said, "And I suspect Mary is attuned to earth. It makes sense."

"You think Miss Anning could have caused the mudslide?" Eliza asked.

"Perhaps on accident," Westing said.

"Hmm." Eliza was skeptical. If the girl used her attunement to find fossils, she might have accidentally pushed too hard, but it seemed like something she would already be skilled at.

"Should we forego the assembly tonight?" Phoebe whispered.

Westing frowned. "I'm tempted, but I suspect Blackerby would tell us we're more likely to learn something if we go."

Phoebe nodded, and Eliza couldn't decide if she looked nervous or relieved.

Westing's party retired to private rooms at the Royal Lion. They had brought changes of clothing for the ball, and even though it was early, Eliza was happy to exchange the damp, sandy muslin hem that flapped against her ankles for the crisp folds of her silk evening gown. The soft purple flattered her and complemented Amethyst's scales. A little work to tame her windblown curls, and she looked like the heiress she was. Perfect for catching some air-headed dandy lord who would terrify her father into relinquishing her freedom. It was a good plan. She smiled at her reflection, but the expression looked forced. Uncertain. Amethyst jumped to her shoulder and nuzzled her ear, restoring her confidence. She harrumphed at the mirror and turned her back on it to return to their private parlour.

Westing and Phoebe hadn't descended yet, and Parry stood alone by the bay window, watchful as always, though he had changed to evening dress. He would have packed away his captain's uniform after his forced retirement, but he wore a coat of deep navy blue instead of black, which Eliza approved of because it was especially fetching on him, and his white pantaloons hinted at well-muscled legs without making his false limb too obvious. It was easy for Eliza to see Parry as nothing more than an extension of her father's control at times, but she was suddenly aware of him as a rather dashing man. Whom she was alone with. She took a step back toward the stairs, and he turned at the rustle of her gown.

He bowed a greeting, his good eye sweeping her gown with an unmistakable look of approval. Perhaps even admiration. Eliza's chest felt tight, her heart beating too fast when their gazes met. This was Captain Parry, the trustee whose yoke she wished to be free of. But she took a step toward him, not quite sure what she was doing or what she wished to say.

Parry straightened and wet his lips, looking about the room as though he needed an escape. Eliza paused, hurt and a bit insulted by his wary expression. Had she made herself such an ogress to him?

"You must be in need of refreshment," he said quickly. "I shall order something for all of us."

And with that, he fled the room, leaving Eliza alone. She scowled after him.

"Why must he be so odious?" she asked Amethyst.

The dragon hopped down and bounded across the room to look out the bow window where Parry had been watching. Eliza followed her companion. One side of the window allowed her a glimpse of the sea, while the other let her watch the comings and goings at the Three Cups. At first, she watched idly, but then she realized she knew some of the people milling in the crowd. The bright red hair, fashionably arranged, could only belong to Lady Amelia Sharp, and where she went... Yes, there was Lady Millicent Blanchfield, her dragon wearing a collar that sparkled with paste jewels.

"We could have done without their company," Eliza mumbled to Amethyst, and the dragon grumbled in what she took for agreement.

Lady Amelia was odd, but it was Lady Millicent who looked down her nose at Eliza as new money and new blood and set Eliza's hackles on end.

But if Lady Millicent was in Lyme Regis, perhaps her brother, Lord Randolph Blanchfield, had come along as well. Now there was a pompous scoundrel who deserved to learn a lesson. And the eldest son of the Earl of Greenley, so not someone Eliza's father would dare forbid from marrying her. Randolph Blanchfield had shown an interest in Eliza—or at least in Eliza's fortune. And Lady Millicent hated to see her brother dangling after new money. Eliza grinned and scratched Amethyst's back.

"Why don't we see if we can turn the tables on Lord Blanchfield?" she whispered.

Amethyst flicked her tale and arched her back in a stretch.

The stair creaked, and Eliza spun to see Phoebe and Westing enter the room, both splendid in their finery.

"Captain Parry has gone to fetch us some refreshment," Eliza said.

A smile brightened Phoebe's tired eyes. "He's always so thoughtful, isn't he?"

There was a hint of teasing in her voice, but Eliza ignored it. No matter how handsome Parry might be, her father would forbid an alliance with him. He wasn't titled or wealthy or powerful. Her father might consider him competent to be her trustee, but he would never let him be her husband. And that was putting aside the fact that Parry was expert at getting her hackles up. Even if he did care for her, which she doubted, they would never suit.

A flurry of voices outside drew her attention to the door of the parlor. A maid knocked and, upon being instructed to enter, poked her head in.

"Begging your pardons," she said, "I'm sorry to intrude, but—"

"Oh, stand aside!" said an imperious female voice. "I would not be one to intrude—not for all the world—but they will never call my arrival an intrusion."

Eliza pinched the bridge of her nose and shared an exasperated look with Phoebe before everyone put on their most polite expression and Lady Millicent pushed her way past the maid.

"My dear Westing!" she exclaimed, taking Lord Westing's hand. "I knew it must be you when I heard the party described. And are you come to Lyme Regis to grace the assembly?" Her gaze swept the room, and perhaps counting the ratio of men and women and finding them not to her liking, she frowned.

"We are," Westing said. "What brings you here?"

"Oh, London is such a bore this time of year, and I told Amelia so, so we settled it that we should go somewhere more pleasant for a few months. Not somewhere too crowded, you understand. And Randolph and I are related by marriage to Lady Sophie, and she is always so glad to have us visit, poor lonely old thing. Oh, and here is Amelia, now! And my brother and his friend Mr. Hackett."

These worthies entered the room and bowed to the assembly there. Mr. Hackett had a long face and prominent teeth that reminded Eliza of a donkey. Lord Blanchfield gave Eliza a very particular smile, and she returned one of her own. The snare was set.

"How long are you staying in Lyme?" Phoebe asked the men.

"As long as it entertains us, eh Hackett?" Lord Blanchfield said, his eyes still on Eliza.

"As long as there's good sport in the country." Hackett gave a braying laugh.

Parry chose that moment to reenter the room, and his eyes widened at the sound. Eliza had to smother a giggle. Lady Millicent gave Parry an appraising look, lingering for a moment on his eye patch, then turned her back on him.

"You will have to dine with us, of course," Westing said. It sounded more like resignation than an invitation, but the newcomers all looked delighted by the prospect.

"And of course, you will show us the town before the assembly," Lady Millicent said. "Since you must know it so well."

Eliza's party exchanged glances.

"In truth," Phoebe said, "We have had a trying morning."

"So we heard!" Hackett exclaimed. "Saving some little wench from the waves. The locals give Captain Parry most of the credit." He raised a quizzing glass to study Parry. "That must be you."

Parry acknowledged this with a nod, more cool than usual. "Indeed, the rumors are mistaken, though. It was Lady Westing and Miss Prescott who brought the child to safety."

"I refuse to believe that Lord Westing had no part in it," Millicent cooed.

Westing raised an eyebrow. "I was unfortunate enough to have missed most of the excitement."

The maid entered with the refreshments Parry had ordered, ending that uncomfortable line of questioning. After they had sampled the sandwiches and tea, Lady Millicent smiled and clapped her hands together.

"Well, no matter what adventures you had this afternoon," Lady Millicent said, "I am convinced the ladies will be more than willing to join us, even if the men are not so sporting."

Phoebe cast a resigned look at Eliza.

"Of course," Eliza said drily. "How could we let anything distract us from shopping?"

"Just so!" Lady Millicent said.

Parry sighed, and Lady Amelia's eyes twinkled. Eliza had to keep from laughing. She didn't quite know what to make of Lady Amelia.

She and Lady Millicent had been at school together, but Lady Amelia seemed to have too much sense to tolerate Lady Millicent for long. There was a hint of humor in Lady Amelia's eyes, however, that made Eliza suspect that the copper-haired lady found amusement where otherwise she might be driven to distraction.

"We should accompany you!" Lord Blanchfield said.

"As if we need men cluttering up our talk," Millicent said, though she cast an inviting glance at Mr. Hackett.

He did not take the bait.

"Oh, let the women go, Randolph! We'll have enough of them at the ball tonight. Lord Westing can tell us the best places for hunting in the district. I wager we can pass the afternoon merrily enough over hounds and horses."

With that terrible threat hanging over them, the woman made a quick exit. Better to giggle over ribbons than be bored to tears hearing a man boast about his favorite hounds. Eliza had never seen much appeal in the hunting sports, though she knew some ladies rode along with the men.

She was surprised to find Captain Parry walking along with them, hanging behind enough to give them space but close enough that it was clear he was chaperoning. Eliza supposed he didn't care for hunting either.

"Do you have a fancy for new ribbons, Captain?" Eliza said.

"Perhaps I do," was all Parry would reply.

As Eliza could not goad him into sparring with her, and he seemed inclined to hang back, Eliza joined the others in their shopping. Parry's silent presence troubled her. Did he think that there was some kind of trouble afoot? He didn't even object to her spending too much on a fan printed with the steps of a popular new quadrille, which was a sign of how distracted he must be.

Once the ladies finished picking up ribbons, gloves, and other trinkets, the sun was low and it was time to return to the Royal Lion. Westing looked nearly bored enough to kill, and he was tracing icy patterns on the arm of his chair. He shot Parry a cutting look. Parry affected an innocent expression and turned to Eliza.

But Randolph Blanchfield was there first.

"I understand the assembly rooms are only a short stroll down the street," he said. "Surely you will allow me to escort you."

"Of course," Eliza said, smiling sweetly.

Parry ended up squiring Lady Amelia, and Mr. Hackett guided a chatting Lady Millicent down the high street to the assembly rooms.

The surf pounded the rocks below the promenade, but the assembly rooms shone like a lighthouse, the windows warm and inviting in the damp chill. Eliza was almost too tired to enjoy the thought of dancing. But the lively music and spicy punch gave her new fortitude, and she was quickly engaged for several dances, including one with Lord Blanchfield and another with Mr. Hackett.

The country assembly was a much less formal affair than a London ball. Westing and Blanchfield's parties were the fashion leaders, though several other members of the *ton*, refugees from the London Season, were in attendance along with the families of well-to-do merchants and gentlemen farmers. Eliza was pleased that her darker features had no noticeable effect on the people present. Many young men asked her to dance, and only Lady Millicent seemed displeased with her.

That was only amplified when Lord Blanchfield paid her particular attention, bringing her punch and making certain she did not lose her shawl, though the room was warm enough. His conversation was shallow, but after dancing with Mr. Hackett and listening to him ramble on about his horses—luckily never pausing long enough for Eliza to respond—she welcomed Blanchfield's banal comments on the roads and weather of Lyme Regis.

"Oh, no!" exclaimed a male with a heavy French. "I cannot bear to stand too close to the windows. The waves will swallow me!"

Eliza gave a start and turned to see Pierre Moreau among the dancers. She had last seen the refugee from Napoleon's reign when his party was overrun by anti-magic Luddites. He had swooned. He showed no embarrassment now, however, as he circulated among the guests, charming them with his heavy accent.

Lord Blanchfield distracted her from the site of Moreau by taking the seat beside her, blocking her view of the Frenchman.

"You are visiting Lord Westing, I gather?" he asked. "Staying at Westing Hall?"

"Yes, Lady Westing invited me."

"It's pleasant to have good connections. You don't find yourself vacationing at the common inn."

"I suppose that is true," Eliza said. "Though good company, I think, makes up for whatever lodgings a person might have."

Blanchfield smiled at her, "That I'm certain we do agree on. I can tell you; I'm finding myself enjoying this seaside visit more now that I have such pleasant company."

Eliza wasn't certain how to respond to such a rehearsed-sounding compliment. Blanchfield spared her the trouble.

"Do you know," he whispered, "My sister only wanted to come here because there are fewer ladies to contend with? I don't think the competition in London suits her."

Eliza found herself blushing for Lady Millicent's sake. "London can be unpleasant."

"Certainly not for you! You were the toast of the town for your debut. The striking beauty from the West Indies. Just the right combination of mystery and knowledge put out about you. But I think you did right not to take the first lures that were cast for you. Your patience will pay off in the end."

Luckily, another lady claimed him for the next dance, and Eliza didn't have to think how to reply. Did he think that she had been playing a game with him in London? How revolting. And yet, she was playing a game with him now.

And wasn't he what she had come to England to find: a wealthy, titled husband who would give her great consequence? And great social freedom? She could not imagine loving Randolph Blanchfield— or him loving her in return—but would she find a gentleman of the *haut ton* who was better? Some of the gentlemen of her acquaintance like Max Hart and Lord Westing were good men, but she could not imagine herself settled happily with any like them.

There were too many ladies in the room that night, and Eliza was grateful enough to miss the next dance. She found Parry watching the dancers with a half-frown masking his thoughts.

"You should not be standing aside when there are young ladies who are not dancing," she reprimanded him.

He gave her a look that she could not read, but there were lines of weariness in his face. She immediately regretting teasing him when she thought of the day he'd had.

"I do see a lady who should be dancing," he said.

Eliza felt a faint pang and wondered who had caught his attention. But he held out his hand for her. Amethyst hopped away to look out the window at the sea, as if giving her permission for the dance.

Eliza met his gaze.

"You are tired," she said. "I should not have teased you."

"Nonsense. A captain is never too tired to enjoy a waltz with a lovely lady."

She took his hand, and he put a hand on her waist, pulling her close and holding her there for a moment. His gaze traveled her face to her lips and then down to that spot on her throat where her pulse beat rapidly.

"You're practically a pirate," she said in a breathy voice. "Do not forget, I know you West Indies captains and cannot be fooled as easily as some London miss."

He smiled enigmatically and met her gaze again, fixing her with his sharp, grey eye. "I do not forget, Miss Prescott."

With that, he twirled her onto the dance floor. The suddenness of the movement startled Eliza, and her instinct was to fight him, but that was not her role in the dance. She relaxed and let Parry guide her, his steps sure and his hand warm and firm on her back. He spun them close to the huge windows overlooking the waves crashing below, and Eliza felt as though they were gliding over the water, the foam of the sea dancing with them. She forgot everything but the heat of Parry so close to her, the intensity of his gaze on her face, and the pull of the tides around her.

Parry brought them to a stop.

"Why aren't we dancing?" Eliza asked dizzily.

"The music ended, love," he said, his voice low.

"Oh, did it?" All she heard was the rhythmic pounding of the waves, and she could dance to those all night.

"Miss Prescott!" Lord Blanchfield's voice drained the warmth from her cheeks.

He bowed to Parry. "What a charming trustee you are, instructing your charge in the waltz. But is it really proper, do you think?" He took a pinch of snuff and smirked at Parry.

Amethyst leaped back onto Eliza's shoulder. The dragon made a rumbling noise and spit hot water into the snuff box.

Lord Blanchfield snarled and dumped out the ruined snuff. The powder swirled in the air before settling to the floor, and a hint of a bitter, burned coffee scent tickled Eliza's nose. Lord Blanchfield schooled his features and snapped the ornate snuff box shut. He held out his hand for Eliza.

Eliza's instinct was to shrink closer to Parry, seek shelter from Randolph Blanchfield and his ilk. But Parry released her with a stiff bow and stepped back.

She took Lord Blanchfield's offered arm automatically, trained from a young age to good manners and good impressions, but as Lord Blanchfield guided her away, she couldn't help glancing back over her shoulder to see Parry watching her go, his weary frown much deeper than before.

Chapter Ten

THE NEXT MORNING, Parry woke feeling as foolish as a hungover midshipman. He should not have danced with Eliza. Miss Prescott. He had been weary, she had been stunning, and that disgusting Randolph Blanchfield had been ogling her, but Parry was a man. He could and must control himself. He had no great social credit, and he was her trustee. People would talk. He didn't care much what they said about him, but he would not have Miss Prescott's name dragged through the gossip gutters.

He dressed and found his way downstairs. Quiet still reigned over the house, which didn't surprise him. They had been out late. Westing was in the study with some local men. Parry went to the dining room, knowing that he would soon hear whatever news the men brought.

Phoebe had found her way to the dining room as well before Westing joined them, his eyes tired. He sat heavily beside Phoebe, and she rubbed his shoulder.

"Still no luck with the unidentified man?" Parry asked.

"None. It's as if he just materialized out of the Channel."

"Or from across it," Parry said.

"French spies?" Westing asked.

Parry nodded, and Westing swore quietly.

Phoebe's eyes looked strained, too. Her uncle was an undersecretary for the Alien Office, and she probably did not relish the idea of their quiet little section of the coast being overrun by spies and counterspies, not to mention extra attention being paid to the dowager viscountess, who was Greek.

"On the bright side," Parry said, cutting a piece of cold chicken, "your local fishermen may be more helpful against foreigners than they would have been with local smugglers. After all, French spies bring too much attention to their own activities."

"True," Westing said. "But how can we confirm they're spies?"

"You're thinking about it backwards," Parry said. "We need to spread the idea around that there could be French spies and then let the fisherman be on the watch. They'll see more than we would."

"But why spy here?" Phoebe asked, her voice rising a note in distress. "What could they want?"

"Lyme is still an important port," Westing said. "And the Duke of Monmouth once launched an invasion from the beach now named after him. He was linked to a water dragon, which helped, of course, but the French might try to follow his example."

Parry shook his head. "Monmouth only succeeded because he had local support. No, the best information we have is that Billy George was asking questions about dragons. We know the French would like to see them destroyed."

"See us destroyed," Westing said icily.

Eliza stepped into the dining room; her eyes wide. "What has happened?"

Phoebe reached a hand for her. "Nothing. We were just speculating. About the dead man."

Eliza gave a wan smile. "Such a topic for breakfast!"

Phoebe chuckled weakly, and they fell into more mundane topics. Parry's mind stayed on Westing's implied question: Were the French interested in Westing specifically? Perhaps it had something to do with his previous run-in with Shaw.

They had barely finished breakfast when young Jamie bounded into the room smelling of sea air.

"I've a message from town, my lord," he said.

Westing grimaced. "No doubt we will be hosting those young scoundrels Lady Millicent brought with her."

"Oh, no, 's not them flash coves," Jamie said. "From that girl with the dead animals. Fostels, they call them."

"Fossils, you young urchin," Westing said. "I know you can speak better than you're choosing to."

Jamie grinned, the picture of innocence, and Phoebe laughed—the first time any of them had really laughed that morning.

Westing snatched the note from him and read it. "Miss Anning would like a word with us as soon as possible."

"Is she well enough?" Phoebe asked.

"It seems. Or, at least, she thinks this is urgent."

"Then we should go," Phoebe said. "I wish I knew where Max was, though. I haven't seen him since yesterday."

Westing put an arm around her shoulder, his brow creased with worry. Parry was worried, too. He didn't believe Max would have anything to do with Shaw or French spies, but the young man was clearly hiding something, and there were too many secrets in the air now.

They made the trip into Lyme Regis and found Mary Anning sitting up in her parlor, her foot bandaged. Her reddish dragon sat on alert next to her, a bit of soil clinging to his claws.

"Miss Anning!" Phoebe said. "Are you feeling well enough to be up and about?"

Mary Anning gave her the look someone might to a child. "I hurt my ankle. It's not like I had the pox or something. Anyway, I've been thinking over what happened, and I think I need to tell all to... to someone who has more influence than me. Like Lord Westing."

Westing nodded. "Go ahead, we're ready to listen."

"I need to do more than tell you. I'm not sure you'll understand unless I show you. Out on the beach."

"You're sure you can make the trip out there?" Phoebe asked.

"Nothing broken, and the swelling has gone down."

Parry noted that she hadn't actually answered the question, but Westing gestured for Mary to lead them. The girl took up a crutch and guided them to the beach. She struggled a bit on the sand, but her lips were pressed in determination. Parry admired her resolve not to let an injury slow her down.

"Would you like us to lease a boat?" Westing asked.

Mary considered this then shook her head. "I think it's maybe something that's dangerous if people know about it. That's what I'm hoping you'll tell me."

So, they walked east, Mary wrestling her crutch over the rocky spots but not complaining. Finally, they reached the landslide. Mary stopped and studied it with a wary expression.

"It warn't natural." She gave them a defiant look. "I'm not just saying that. I saw someone up there just before it happened. I didn't think much of it—just a gentleman out for a stroll—but then there was a noise and suddenly the cliff was coming down on me."

"Did he see you down here?" Westing asked.

"I can't be sure, but I think so. I've been thinking that he was looking for me, in fact."

With that, they picked their way over the rocks to the other side, Westing lending Mary his arm.

"It's just this way," Mary said. "I wasn't sure at first, but Sandy and me, we've seen enough of it now."

Eliza glanced at the girl's red dragon. "You are attuned to earth? With your dragon?"

Mary pursed her lips. "I don't know all the 'ficial words for it, but with Sandy around, it's easy for me to dig, and he seems to be able to help me find things no one else sees."

"You know," Westing said, "we could teach you more about being dragon-linked. How to use your abilities. You could enjoy more social advantages."

Mary regarded him narrowly. "Meaning no disrespect, your lordship, but my Pa used to say that London and its people are wicked, and I should stay away from all that lot."

Westing looked a little chagrined, and Parry laughed out loud.

"Anyway, we're here."

Mary gestured to the side of the cliff where she had been excavating. It took Parry a moment, but then he saw protruding from the soil in places the outline of a large skull—much larger than any other he had seen. Some ancient sea creature, perhaps, with a reptile body.

Eliza gasped, and then Parry saw the rest of it: the wings, the tail, the claws. This was the skeleton of an adult dragon.

"What does it mean?" Phoebe asked in a breathy whisper.

Westing stared up at the skeleton, saying nothing.

"It means dragons are not as immortal as we thought," Parry said quietly.

He gingerly reached out to touch the darkened bones—actual bones, he was sure, not ancient enough to be fossils.

"It's huge," Eliza said. "It must have been very elderly. Did it die of old age, do you think?"

"Possible," Parry said. "Maybe once dragons live out their life, they return to the dust. Dust thou art, and unto dust thou shalt return.'"

"But it is possible..." Westing said, his voice grave. "It is possible that they can also be killed."

"What do you suppose happens when they die?" Phoebe asked. "They're linked to the health of the land."

"Yes." Westing's brow furrowed. "There are stories that there was once a great catastrophe along this coast."

"You think that's what killed the dragon?" Phoebe gripped his arm.

"Or, it's what happens when a dragon dies."

"But what could have killed it?" Eliza asked, cradling Amethyst protectively.

"There's probably no way to know at this late date," Parry said. "I think the more pertinent question for us at this moment is, who wanted to keep this a secret? Because I think we know why someone tried to silence Miss Anning."

They all stared again at the remains.

"Someone who wants to protect dragons? Doesn't want people to know they can die?" Phoebe asked quietly.

"Or," Parry said, "someone who is glad they can die, but doesn't want us to know."

"Why must you always assume the worst?" Eliza snapped.

"Because I can't defend against the worst if I don't anticipate it." Parry paced; his gait uneven in the sand as he studied the dragon bones from another angle. "If an enemy wanted to attack England, what more devastating way than by attacking her dragons?"

Westing nodded slowly. "And all the more devastating if we don't expect it. Don't know to guard against it."

"But we still don't know how to guard against it," Phoebe said. "We don't know how they can be killed, so how can we protect them?"

Eliza folded her arms. "We also don't know if anything other than extreme old age can cause this." She shuddered. "We don't even know that this dragon is completely dead. What if its essence is still lingering in there?"

Parry tapped on the bone. "I doubt it. It feels dead. The important thing is, we need to know who tried to hide Miss Anning's discovery if we're going to learn why they did it."

Westing turned to the girl. "Did anyone else know about this find?"

"No. I wanted to keep it secret then sell it to some museum or something in London."

"But someone could have followed you," Parry said.

She shrugged ruefully. "People know I'm good at finding fossils. I'm pretty slippery, but maybe someone could have followed."

Westing looked grim. "Can you remember anything about the person you saw?"

Her brow furrowed. "It was a man. Not just because of the clothes. He walked like a man."

"Did you see how he made the earth move?"

"No, but I heard a loud noise just a moment before."

Parry nodded. "More likely some kind of explosive than dragon magic, then."

"We'll need to investigate the top of the landslide," Westing said, his face pale.

Westing wanted to take Mary home, but she insisted on coming with them.

"I understand the earth. I might be able to discover something you cannot."

That was hard to argue with, so they all helped each other up the slope to the site of the landslide. There was a solid chunk of earth torn away, as if a giant claw had scraped it down into the sea.

"Yes, this wasn't natural," Westing said. "And it wasn't magic."

Parry nodded his agreement. "I see traces of gunpowder over here. That also means this wasn't something that happened without forethought. Someone was planning this."

"Miss Anning was their target," Westing said, his voice low so as not to carry to the girl.

"It would be an awfully strong coincidence if she wasn't. It was meant to look like an accident. Maybe to make her disappear forever. They either wanted to cover up her find or claim it for themselves. I think whomever did this did not have a dragon—and they didn't reckon on one warning Mary."

"Could it have been unrelated to the dragon bones entirely?" Westing asked.

Parry hesitated. "It's possible. But then you have to ask why else someone would want to harm the child."

They glanced over at Mary examining the edge where the rocks had slid away.

"Miss Anning," Westing called. "Can you tell us if there's anyone you know of that might want to hurt you? Someone who dislikes you or your family?"

She looked thoughtful. "Not really. We mostly keep to ourselves. Just trying to get by."

"Has anyone ever threatened you before?"

Her eyes widened a little and she shook her head. "No, sir. I mind my business and they mind theirs."

"No one bothered you before you found the dragon bones," Parry said. It wasn't a question.

"Could you have let word slip about what you found?" Westing asked.

Again, she looked thoughtful, and again she shook her head. "No one, sir. Not even Mum. I wasn't sure myself at first, so I didn't think I ought to say anything."

"Could there be a naturalist who wanted it but didn't want to pay for it?" Phoebe asked.

"She hasn't told anyone yet," Eliza reminded her.

Parry shook his head. "We know Shaw wants dragons dead. It's too much like coincidence, and I don't trust them."

Westing sighed. "Neither do I. Miss Anning, we'll see you safely home. I want you to keep a sharp eye out. Watch out for yourself, and tell me immediately if anyone starts asking questions about dragon bones. I'll have the constable keep a closer watch on your street."

"Yes, sir."

Mary Anning looked frightened. Parry didn't blame her.

Chapter Eleven

IMAGES OF DRAGON bones haunted Eliza every time she closed her eyes. And nightmares of England reduced to rubble, its dragon-linked destined for the guillotine. After tossing and turning for hours, she threw off her blankets and decided to head down to the library for something to read. Not Miss Charity's latest book. She didn't have the patience to see herself parodied as fool at the moment. No, something familiar and reassuring. She'd always been fond of Shakespeare's *The Tempest*, and she was sure Westing had a copy.

She fumbled her way down the stairs with only the dim light of a candle. One of the footmen was asleep by the front door. Not much of a guard, but at least if someone broke in, they would likely trip over the man.

The library was peaceful and dark. She held up the candle, casting long shadows like grasping fingers over the spines of the books. Phoebe had said something about half the library being in London, but a century of books would leave something for her to read. Many of these looked quite old: journals, account books, and such. That might help put her to sleep.

She set her candle down and reached for one of the books. Amethyst's head snapped around to stare at the window. The dragon made an odd clicking noise in her throat. Eliza quickly snuffed the candle and snuck to the window. Something moved in the shadows outside. No. Someone. The shadows seemed to close in around Eliza, and her breath came faster.

The wise thing would be to get the men, but the intruder was likely to get away by the time they came downstairs, so Eliza tightened her dressing gown and snuck out of the library.

As she made her way quietly to the garden doors, she tried to buoy up her courage. She wasn't going to confront the criminal, just spy out who they were and what they were doing. It wasn't safe, precisely, but she would keep her distance, and Amethyst would protect her. The dragon was a reassuring weight on her shoulder, head up and reptilian eyes alert as Eliza slipped into the darkness.

She stayed close to the house. Close to where someone would hear if she screamed. The moon was down, clouds covered the stars, and the darkness hung heavy over the gardens, almost something she could feel on her skin. She took a deep breath, trying not to imagine she was inhaling the night. But the air was thick and cloying. It seemed like more than sea mist. It seemed like—

"Blackerby," she hissed under her breath.

"I hope you're not taking my name in vain," said a mocking voice nearby.

Eliza jumped, and Amethyst hissed and flapped her wings. "Well, I ought to! I thought you were a thief or a murderer!"

"You sound a little disappointed." The Earl of Blackerby stepped forward, trailing wisps of deep black from his tall, lean frame like a kraken's tentacles. His teeth flashed in the dark. "If I killed someone, would you be happy to see me?"

"Of course not."

"Ah, then it was a *particular* thief or murderer you were sneaking out to meet?"

Eliza gasped in indignation. "Of all the ridiculous things to say. I only wanted to prove to… to certain people that I could… well, that my eyes are as sharp as anyone's. I wasn't going to let any harm come to anyone in this house."

"Very noble of you. And you were going to apprehend this thief-murderer with your bare hands? Quite brave."

"I was going to raise the hue and cry. And let Amethyst loose on them. And I still might. What are you doing here? I don't believe Lord Westing knows you're about."

"No, he does not. But I don't need his permission to investigate matters of national safety." His shadows circled them like hungry hounds. "Since you are already compromising your reputation by this clandestine conversation with me, won't you stay a moment and tell me what you know about the dragon skeleton?"

That tripped her up for a moment, but she said, "What dragon skeleton?"

"You are a lovely little liar. Not very convincing, though."

"How would you know about any dragon skeleton?"

Blackerby's low chuckle slithered through the night. "Miss Prescott, it is my business to know such things."

Eliza's eyes narrowed. The only people who knew about the dragon were Miss Anning, the party at Westing Park, and whoever tried to kill Miss Anning. "I don't feel inclined to tell you anything."

"Very well. I doubt you know more than I have already gleaned anyway."

Eliza rolled her eyes. "You won't goad me into telling you more, especially not with cheap tricks like that."

Another chuckle. "How spirited of you. If you're not here to help me, however, might I suggest you would be better off out of the way of my investigation?"

Eliza wanted to refuse, just to avoid letting the obnoxious earl order her about, but she couldn't think of a reason to stay, so she huffed and marched back into the house.

~

Eliza woke the next morning wondering if she had dreamed the encounter with Blackerby. If not, though, she would of course warn Westing that he was about. She dressed and headed down to the dining room. Her hopes for breakfast were entirely ruined to find Lord

Blackerby sharing the table with her hosts. Phoebe chatted politely with him, Max Hart—the prodigal returned—watched him warily, and Westing looked like he would have been just as happy to toss the meddlesome earl out a window. Eliza could sympathize. Only Captain Parry ate his breakfast with apparent equanimity.

"Well, my dear Miss Prescott," Blackerby purred. "What a delightful surprise."

She smirked at him and sat farther down the table. But not so far that she couldn't eavesdrop. Amethyst hissed at the earl's deep gray dragon and hopped on the table beside Eliza.

"I understand your concern," Westing said to the earl. "We also considered that Shaw might be interested in the findings. But I can't rule out other possibilities. Several crimes have been committed, and I want to be sure the right person is held accountable."

"As do I. But I have one more fact to add to your consideration. Deborah Shaw is missing."

Max choked on his toasted roll. Eliza drew a deep breath. Deborah was Shaw's niece, a dragon-linked girl attuned to lightning whom Shaw very much wanted to use against England. Phoebe had protected the girl once, but Eliza was under the impression that Miss Shaw had since been under Blackerby's watchful eye.

Phoebe dropped her fork. "Missing? Why didn't you say so at once?"

"Do you know where she is?" Blackerby toyed with his quizzing glass.

"No." Phoebe looked shocked.

"I suspected as much. Therefore, immediately alarming you with that news served no purpose."

Phoebe scowled at him. "She might be in danger. We have to find her."

"I have reason to hope she has not fallen into the clutches of her nefarious uncle," Blackerby said. "It appears she left of her own accord. Er, climbed out a window by tying together her bedsheets."

Phoebe sat back with a groan, though Eliza detected a faint smile on her lips. "Of course she did. But Shaw could have captured her since then."

"Possible. But I think the girl clever in her own fashion and unlikely to have put herself in his way."

"True," Phoebe said. "Oh, foolish Deborah! What are you planning?" To Blackerby she said, "Do you have any indication of where or why she went?"

"Oh, she left a note for her aunt."

He produced the letter from a pocket in his coat. Phoebe read it, her lips occasionally quirking in amusement, but at the end she set it aside and rolled her eyes. "She is a very dramatic girl, but she claims that Rahab led her away. Have you ever heard of such a thing?"

"Dragons might occasionally warn their humans of danger. It's possible."

Eliza glanced at Amethyst. Had there been times that the dragon was trying to warn her of something? Certainly, Amethyst had alerted her to Blackerby's presence the night before. She wished she could believe it was her little friend and not the sea that spoke of danger to her mind, but she did not.

"We will watch for Deborah," Phoebe said. "She would have to be resourceful to find her way here, though."

"And you don't think Miss Shaw is resourceful?" Max said resentfully.

"She is," Phoebe admitted. "That is what worries me. It is not exactly safe for a girl to be wandering around the area alone."

Max shrugged one shoulder but looked satisfied with his sister's answer.

"None of you have seen any sign of her, then?" Blackerby asked.

They all shook their heads.

"How disappointing. And I expected you to be right in the heart of the action. I hope marriage is not making you dull, Westing."

Westing curled a lip at that, and Parry snorted in amusement.

"Dragon bones aren't enough for you?" Parry asked.

"They won't be enough for our enemy," Blackerby reminded him. "At least, not just one set."

"I suppose you'll be wanting a guest room?" Westing asked Blackerby.

"I would hate to impose on you, dear Westing. No, I will be staying with Lady Sophie. I am given to understand she loves company, and I find the situation there... lively."

Eliza had to contain a smile. She was certain it was lively, with that many unhappy people under one roof. And plenty of gossip, which Blackerby would like.

"That explains it, then," Westing said.

"Explains what?" Blackerby asked with a faint smile, as if he already knew.

"Why Lady Sophie has invited us all to a card party this evening and as well as dinner later this week. I thought she was being extraordinarily social. I imagine she needed someone to buffer her from all that company. But this is not your first visit to Westing Hall, is it?"

"You have never invited me in the past," Blackerby said. "And your father was never so hospitable."

"You were skulking around the other night, too," Eliza said.

Blackerby raised a hand to his chest. "My dear, I never skulk!"

Parry glanced down at Blackerby's boots and nodded. "Long strides."

Westing's eye narrowed. "You were here before any of us knew about the dragon bones, then."

"I admit, the dragon bones are an interesting development, but, no, anytime I lose one of my agents, it warrants my personal attention."

Parry leaned forward, pointing at Blackerby with his fork. "Then the men in the boat *were* spies—they were working for you!"

Blackerby feigned a clap. "Bravo. And I am quite upset to have lost them." He smiled, all shark-like teeth. "But I will find whomever cut their throats and return the favor."

"We will find them," Westing said. "But we will have to work together. No more secrets. No more skulking in the shadows. Or striding in them."

Blackerby laughed. "Very well. You have a deal."

Chapter Twelve

ELIZA COULDN'T SAY she was looking forward to Lady Sophie's card party. Not with Blackerby and possibly Shaw lurking about somewhere. And the thought of flirting with Randolph Blanchfield made her stomach turn. But this was her plan—her path to freedom from her father's ridiculous strictures. He had too much pride and savvy to want to see his daughter paired with a fool who would fritter away her money, even if the fool was heir to an earldom. She just had to prove that to him, set the gossip of her terrible, empty-headed match flying all the way back to Dominica. Then, her father would withdraw his demand that a man be in control of her fortune. He would let Eliza take the reins and control her own fate.

She put extra time into arranging her hair on the day of the party. Randolph Blanchfield had to be lured in, of course. And she wouldn't give Lady Sophie or Lady Millicent any reason to look down on her.

When she finally descended the stairs, Captain Parry was already lounging in the great hall. He always managed to look as masterful as any lord, as though the world were a ship under his command. If her plan went well, maybe someday Eliza would know that feeling, too.

Parry stood when he saw her, and something flashed in his eyes. Admiration? Her cheeks warmed as he bowed and took her hand.

"And who are you out to impress tonight, love?" he asked, his voice low.

Her voice caught in her throat for a moment. Then she smiled. "Everyone, of course."

"Of course," he echoed, a bite in his words.

Eliza pulled her hand away and turned to study a huge painting of some previous Lord Westing, trying to put Captain Parry and his tone out of mind. Why should she care what he thought? He seemed determined to make sure she did not take in London. In two years, she would be twenty-one and allowed to inherit the small fortune left to her by her mother, but that seemed like ages away, and it still did not guarantee that her father would let her have any more funds if she did not marry. He might call her home to Dominica and declare her time in England a waste. Then she would never be free. She could not lose this chance to find her own way.

By the time the carriage rolled away from Westing Park, Eliza was excited and nervous. Phoebe summoned a light to guide them on their way, and it allowed Eliza a good look at Lady Sophie's ancient home when they approached up the long carriage sweep.

After Westing said that Lady Sophie lived in the older family home, Eliza had pictured the elderly lady inhabiting a dilapidated castle. The type with bats and groaning ghosts. Instead, the house had been updated over the years to resemble a more fashionable Palladian manor house, a great rectangular box with understated classical columns and many windows offsetting the fact that parts of it were clearly of an older design. Eliza was a little disappointed.

The footman showed the ladies where they could leave their coats, and Westing escorted Phoebe inside. Eliza latched onto Max's arm before Parry would feel obligated to offer, and they found the card party already in progress. Lady Amelia, Randolph Blanchfield, Lady Millicent, and Mr. Hackett played at vingt-un, while Blackerby engaged in flirting with Lady Sophie.

Lady Sophie waved the party over. "You see, the young people wish to play such noisy games. What do you say, my lord earl, now that we have more players, we can make up sets for whist." A challenging look came into her eyes as she glanced at Eliza. "Unless that is too difficult a game."

"I would be happy to play whist," Eliza said. "I am quite fond of it."

"I, alas, am not," Blackerby said. "But I'm certain Miss Prescott will make an excellent partner for Lady Sophie."

Lady Sophie and Eliza exchanged murderous looks. The earl barely hid his smile behind a handkerchief.

Phoebe jumped in, "I am not very good at whist, but Westing and I will play with you, Lady Sophie."

"Oh, no!" Randolph Blanchfield interjected from his table. "Lady Westing, you must play vingt-un with me."

Phoebe's eyes narrowed, and Eliza remembered her friend's first encounter with Lord Blanchfield, when her uncontrolled magic gave away her cards at piquet. She smirked. "Anytime you wish."

"Well," Max said, "I can count to twenty-one as well as anyone, but don't look to me for whist. Too much to keep track of. Not at all the thing for a restful evening."

Westing shrugged in resignation. "I'll join you for whist, Lady Sophie. And Captain Parry is an excellent player."

"That won't do if Miss Prescott is playing!" Lady Sophie exclaimed. "He is the trustee of Miss Prescott, is he not? He must behave with propriety. One cannot say he is disinterested."

Parry smiled ruefully. "No, one cannot."

"I would be happy to partner with Captain Parry," Lady Amelia said. "If Miss Prescott wishes to take my place at vingt-un."

Lady Amelia smiled at Parry. Her smile was not flirtatious, but Eliza still felt a smolder of resentment and suspected her of having ulterior motivations. And she felt even more resentment against the Earl of Blackerby, whom she suspected played whist perfectly well but looked delighted with the chaos he had caused.

"Excellent," Lady Sophie said. "I will partner with Westing. He is not so good a player as his father, but he will do."

Annoyance flashed over Westing's face at this comparison, but he schooled his features and bowed his assent.

"Eliza," Phoebe called. "Do join Max and I over here."

So, Eliza ended up on one side of Randolph Blanchfield, with Phoebe on the other. Lady Millicent, Mr. Hackett, and Max sat across from her. Eliza realized she should have been pleased with this arrangement, since it gave her just the opportunity she needed to advance her cause with Randolph Blanchfield. He seemed happy as a rooster, flirting with both ladies and not showing his disappointment that Phoebe now controlled her magic well enough that she did not give her cards away. Phoebe had even overcome her foot tapping, so when Eliza's turn came to play the bank, she had difficulty guessing how close her friend's cards were to twenty-one.

When they paused to shuffle the cards and change dealers, Lord Blanchfield turned his attention entirely to Eliza. Lady Millicent scowled at them but consoled herself by flirting with Hackett, leaving Phoebe and Max to exchange comments which Eliza couldn't hear but which made them both laugh.

"Have you walked out to see the fossils?" Eliza asked Lord Blanchfield.

"Oh, my sister dragged me along, and of course one must see them when in Lyme. It's the thing to do. I even bought one. Seems like nothing more than a rock to me, but must be seen doing the fashionable thing."

Eliza's stomach knotted. It reminded her of the kind of thing her father would say. That they were always on display. Always to put on a good face. She grew weary of caring. "I think—"

"You ought to visit my yacht," he cut her off. "Perhaps Westing would bring your party to see it. That captain fellow might give me a few pointers. Don't know much about sailing it, but it's a great thing to have."

Eliza settled back and let her mind wander while he droned on. Randolph Blanchfield didn't care about fossils or Mary Anning or probably anything but himself. He only took an interest in her because of what she would mean to him: an heiress and dragon-linked on top of that. A matrimonial prize. And Randolph Blanchfield liked to win prizes.

Then again, Eliza didn't care for him, either. It made him ideal for this game with her father. Unless, of course, her father approved of

Randolph. She was not interested in marrying the man, but if it were that or return to Dominica to be her father's dress-up doll for the rest of her life? Or marry some awful plantation owner that her father pushed her onto? That she could not abide, living on a plantation. But married to someone like Randolph Blanchfield, she would have a secure social position. With security came the freedom to live her life on her terms. Randolph wouldn't care what she did. Not like her father, who used her as a political pawn. She would be free. That was all she really wanted.

Almost.

She glanced at Parry and quickly looked away.

Love, after all, was a fairy tale. Sweet girls like Phoebe might find it, but Eliza had never been a sweet girl. Too loud. Too assertive. Too much.

So perhaps she would end her days as her mother had, in a safe but distant marriage. Her father was English, but her mother was the West Indies: rich, beautiful, lively. Her father valued her mother, perhaps more for her resources than for any unique quality of herself. Her mother had been a prize, just as Eliza was.

Her father bragged to his associates that Eliza's dragon hinted at a forgotten royal ancestor on his side, but Eliza knew he was wrong because her mother had taught her their legacy of dragon-linked African scholars, Carib queens, Spanish hidalgas, and Jewish explorers. But the sea and the sky had stolen her mother from her in one ferocious storm that had changed bays and inlets, threw trees through walls like spears, and scoured people from the shores. That hurricane had reshaped Eliza's life just as it reshaped the island.

She wished she could shape life the way she wanted it, but it didn't seem possible. Like she was fighting the combined might of the sea and the sky. It was easier to drift along in the stream than to fight to go in a different direction. But did drifting along mean she would float along with someone like Randolph Blanchfield?

She turned her attention on him again. He was pressing her to ask Westing to allow them all to go sailing under his command. She shivered.

"Perhaps some time," she said, trying to be polite, but not committing to anything. That was the key. Don't commit.

They started another round of vingt-un, this time with Lord Blanchfield dealing. Hackett had apparently grown bored with Lady Millicent and tried to tell Eliza about his newest horse, practically shouting across the table while Lady Millicent strove to regain his attention.

Mushroom leapt onto the table and tried to steal a mislaid card from Lady Millicent's dragon, scattering more discards around the table.

Distracted by the noise, Eliza lost count of her cards' values, ending up with more than twenty-one. She sighed and placed her cards down.

Lady Millicent snarled and threw hers onto the table. "You misdealt the cards," she snapped at her brother.

"I did not. You just can't count."

Eliza frowned and looked at her cards again. "No, I think I have more cards than I asked for as well."

Randolph Blanchfield laughed. "Women! So bad with numbers."

Lady Millicent pushed her chair back. "No. I think you are cheating!"

A hush fell over everyone. Randolph Blanchfield's smile stayed frozen on his face, but the color drained from his cheeks, and his eyes glittered dangerously. "Really, sister? Isn't that a bit hysteric? It's just a friendly game after all."

"Hysteric?" she asked coldly. Her dragon hissed and gathered itself as though it would pounce.

"It appears to me," Blackerby said, his deep voice cutting through the tension, "that the moon is setting. It might be safer for all if Westing's party headed home for the night."

Randolph Blanchfield opened his mouth as if he would object, but then he shrugged angrily and returned to glaring at his sister.

Westing stood. "Indeed. Thank you, Lady Sophie, for the... the night of cards."

She nodded, her expression sour as she glared at her cousins-by-marriage.

Eliza was only too glad to extricate herself from the card party and head out into the last of the moonlight. Mist hung over the green hills, heavy and clinging. She pulled her cape tightly around her shoulders, but she couldn't shake off the chill of Lady Sophie's drawing room. England or Dominica, she wasn't sure either place offered her a chance for happiness.

Chapter Thirteen

THE GROUP WAS NOT in a festive mood when they returned to Westing Park. Everyone said curt goodnights and headed for their rooms.

Eliza only partly undressed and sunk into bed, tired but sure she wouldn't be able to sleep. Lord Randolph Blanchfield was a beast. A beast dressed in gentleman's clothing, but a beast nonetheless. She didn't want to even pretend to be interested in him. Would she find anyone better? Hackett perhaps? He was more empty-headed, but not as brutish. Not a lord, but of a good enough family that he could work for her scheme. He might not even realize he was rumored to be courting her as long as he could talk about horses and hounds.

Eliza drifted into dreams of being back in the West Indies in a great golden birdcage where she could see the ocean but never get near it, and her father fed her birdseed from a silver cup.

Amethyst pounced on Eliza's chest, waking her from her sleep. She sat up with a gasp, looking around her dark room in confusion.

"Amethyst!" Eliza scolded.

Danger. The whisper of a thought drifted around her like smoke.

Then she heard the noise. A faint tinkling, like a fall of breaking glass. She scrambled for her dressing gown and raced to look out her window, but of course she could not see directly below her. She ran to the door and threw it open, ready to raise the alarm.

She was not the only one awake, though. A door slammed down the hall, and Westing and Phoebe dashed from their room, encased in an orb of light.

Two rooms down from Eliza, Parry's door opened, and he stepped into the corridor. He stopped and stared at Eliza, and she was suddenly very aware of her undress. And his, wearing only his trousers with his night shirt half tucked in. He has fastened on his false leg, but not the patch over his eye. Eliza had never seen him without it, and she tried not to stare at the cloudy white of his blinded eye. Instead, she found herself studying the broad set of his shoulders and the thick muscles visible through his shirt sleeves. Her face warmed. Not better.

"What happened?" he asked, his voice its usual commanding tone, which made her forget his eye and—mostly—those well-muscled arms.

"Amethyst woke me. I thought I heard a window break."

His expression hardened, and he stepped forward, walking between her and whatever danger lurked downstairs. He held up his pistol. Those broad shoulders seemed as sure as a sea wall breaking apart any threats. It was easy to forget that this man who was so often at her side was also a proficient and deadly fighter.

Max strolled down the corridor, impeccably dressed as if he had been up for hours. Or had never gone to sleep.

"Am I interrupting something?" he asked, eyebrows raised.

Captain Parry grinned. "You ought to be—downstairs, where there's some sort of break in. I'm just making sure my ward is safe."

The words stung Eliza. His ward? Was that what she was? She was certainly no child, even if he thought she was.

They walked downstairs, Parry's pistol at the ready and Max bringing up the rear. When they reached the front hall, the bright light from the library told them where to find Westing and Phoebe.

Westing stood by a broken window, his face red with fury.

"Did you catch him?" Parry asked.

Westing shook his head. "Whoever it was, he fled as soon as he heard us. I have already sent for the constable."

Parry frowned at the broken glass and peered out the window. "Not the easiest access to the house. As if they wanted to get into the library specifically."

Phoebe pointed to one of the shelves where the books had been hastily pulled and dropped. "They were looking for something."

"I don't keep anything valuable in here," Westing said.

"You're assuming it's a common burglar," Parry said.

"You think not?" Westing asked.

"I think not."

"It wasn't!" said a voice from outside. Brainy Jamie's head popped into view.

"Jamie!" Phoebe said. "What are you doing out there?"

"I chased 'im," Jamie said matter-of-factly.

"That's noble, but you needn't put yourself in danger," Westing said.

"No, but it was 'im," Jamie said.

"Who?"

"You know, that bad 'un. Sudbury. Shaw."

"You're sure?" Westing asked.

"He's good at disguising himself," Phoebe reminded him.

"It warn't 'is face I recognized. It was 'is manners. I'm sure. I 'ave an excellent mem'ry."

They looked at each other. Max had gone especially pale, and Eliza wondered why he was more afraid of Shaw than the rest of them.

"I believe the lad," Blackerby said from the darkness of the gardens.

He strolled up behind Jamie, his gait casual but his face unusually serious.

"Is there anyone who isn't in my garden in the middle of the night?" Westing snapped.

"You sent for the constable." Blackerby grinned. "You got me instead. Lucky you."

Westing grimaced. "You think Shaw had a hand in this?"

"I have no proof yet, but it seems most reasonable. So, for the sake of argument, what might Shaw want in your library?"

Westing shrugged helplessly and smoothed back his white-blond hair. "We do have some books on dragons. Their history and habits. It's hard for me to imagine they contain anything Shaw doesn't know."

"Yet something brought him here."

"You don't think he was drawn here by the dragon bones?" Parry asked.

"I think he was drawn to Lyme by them, or at least that they must interest him greatly. But I doubt he would bring attention to himself by breaking into the library at Westing Hall without good reason." Blackerby raised his quizzing glass to study Westing. "It is not unreasonable to suppose that something in your library might hold clues about a dragon that died so near your family estates."

"You think the Westings harbored some secrets about dragons?" Westing looked skeptical, but then his expression softened a little. "It is possible my father knew things that he told my older brother but not me."

"Then I hope everyone enjoys reading," Blackerby said. "Because we have a good many books to sort through. Incidentally, I was beginning to find the company at Lady Sophie's tiresome. I thought I would take you up on your generous offer of a room, at least until her ladyship has finished nagging herself hoarse."

Westing looked like he might have a great deal to say about that, but he only rubbed his eyes. "Very well." He glanced over his shoulder at Baxter, the butler, who appeared to be trying very hard to act as though all of this were normal. "Prepare the yellow room for the earl."

Phoebe gave her husband a wary glance.

The butler cleared his throat. "The... the *yellow* room, my lord?"

Westing grinned wickedly. "Yes, the yellow room."

"Oh, go along," Blackerby said with a dry chuckle. "I'm sure *the yellow room* is dreadful, but as long as it does not include Lady Sophie, it will do. For tonight, we'll be reading instead of sleeping anyway."

～

As dawn approached, Eliza was falling sleep over a book on the anatomy of dragons. Westing and Parry had gone to escort his stepmama and siblings over from the dower house to keep them safe, and Max had followed shortly after. Phoebe's forehead wrinkled in concentration as she tried to decipher old handwriting, and Blackerby had his feet propped up on a table and swung his quizzing glass on its chain as he read.

Joshua came bounding into the room, his eyes bright with excitement.

"Josh! I'm glad you're safe." Phoebe set her book aside. "Has there been trouble at the dowager house?"

"No, it's boring there. Did Mr. Sudbury—er, Shaw—really break into the library?"

"I'm afraid so," Phoebe said.

"He was always interested in West's library in London, too. Sometimes I think he gave me writing exercises just to keep me busy so he could look through the books."

Phoebe and Eliza shared a look.

"Do you remember which books he looked through?" Blackerby asked.

"Some of the most boring ones. Dusty old journals. The only things worse in the whole library were the books about soils." He made a face. "That would only be interesting if I were attuned to earth, and then I probably wouldn't need to read them anyway."

Eliza shook her head at his innocent faith in magic. If only she understood water just by being attuned to it. Maybe Westing had books about the sea.

The viscount had entered the room while Joshua spoke. He frowned to himself, then rang the bell for Baxter. The butler returned, still looking fresh and unflustered.

"Send someone to the townhouse in London to bring back all the old diaries in the library. Someone quick and reliable."

"Yes, my lord," Baxter said with no more concern than if Westing had called for tea.

Phoebe turned her attention back to Joshua. "Did Shaw ever say anything to you about what he was reading?"

"Not really. He quizzed me on history sometimes when he read, asking how old the house is, how long the village had been here, but I didn't know much about it. He said I ought to know more of my own history."

"What kinds of things did he ask about the house?" Westing sat on the sofa by his wife.

"Well, he didn't exactly ask about it. He made me tell him things about our family's history. The Civil War, other people in the family who had been dragon-linked, the old dragon tor—"

"He knows about that?" Phoebe asked.

"Everybody knows about it." Joshua shrugged and snatched up Tom, who had followed him into the library and sprawled across an open book.

"But what did he want to know?" Westing asked.

"How long it had been there. What kind of dragon it is. If anyone ever saw bits of its treasure."

Phoebe looked interested. "Do they?"

"No, ma'am. No one knows anything about the dragon. Not even if it's really there."

Eliza disagreed, but this wasn't the time for that.

"Nobody knows now," Phoebe said. "But maybe they did before." She turned back to the bookshelf. "Help me find any old diaries."

"We have to read them?" Joshua looked horrified.

Phoebe laughed. "I suppose Shaw was right—you do need to learn more about your family history."

She recruited Lady Zoe as well, who protested that her English wasn't excellent but accepted a thin book of hours. Jamie boasted that he couldn't read well yet and was therefore excused to amuse young Alexandria, but everyone else settled down to pore over the old-fashioned handwriting.

Eliza's thoughts drifted to speculations about Shaw, and she almost missed a passage about dragons that was stuffed between accounts of land management during the Civil War.

"This is interesting," she said. "Back in Charles I's time, they tried to study the local dragon. Apparently, it was attuned to earth or metal, and they wanted to see if it could help them in the war." Her forehead wrinkled. "They thought it might be willing. I'm not sure from this if they actually spoke to it or if they were only assuming."

"I want to talk to a dragon," Joshua said wistfully.

"That would be helpful," Phoebe muttered.

Eliza scanned the pages. "The words are a bit blotted. Something about the dragon's hoard." She squinted and tilted her head, willing the smudged, dark brown ink to be more clear. "Something precious to the dragon."

"Were they trying to bribe it?" Phoebe asked.

"Interesting idea," Parry said, striding in from the doorway to look over Eliza's shoulder.

Eliza's thoughts shot away like a startled school of fish, and she was only aware of Parry's warmth hovering behind her as he scanned the book. He reached down to turn the page, his hand brushing hers, and warmth bolted up her arm.

Phoebe looked around the room. "Where's Max?"

Westing's brows drew together. "He's not with you?"

"No, he left shortly after you did. I thought..." Phoebe trailed off, her forehead creased with worry. "Oh, no. Max, what are you doing?"

"In the meantime," Blackerby said, "Captain Parry looks like he's discovered something interesting. Please, don't tease us by keeping us in suspense."

Parry sat close to Eliza, their knees touching, and he gently lifted the book from her hands. Her mouth felt dry, her stomach fluttery, and she didn't object.

"There may be something here that explains the skeleton in the cliff," Parry said. "It's not spelled out clearly, but we can read between the lines. They did talk to the dragon, and he wasn't interested in helping with their war. He was a very old dragon, or at least it sounds that way. He didn't care much about anything outside of his stretch of the coast. Human wars pass with the centuries, after all."

"The dragon told them this?" Westing asked.

"They had some way of communicating with it, at least."

"Wonderful!" Joshua said.

"It's not just a rumor, then," Blackerby said. "I know of no such thing that occurs in our times."

"I think I know why," Eliza said, gathering her distracted thoughts enough to read along with Parry. "The humans didn't accept the dragon's answer. They wanted to make it fight for them."

Westing squeezed his eyes shut. "We have always been a headstrong lot."

Eliza went on. "They discovered something—it's not clear what—but some way to force the dragon to obey them. But..."

"Yes?" Blackerby urged.

"But when they tried, it killed the dragon," Parry finished.

Blackerby clamped his hand shut on his quizzing glass. "How? Does it say how they tried to control it?"

Parry narrowed his eyes. "Why are you so anxious to know?"

"Do you mistrust my intentions?" Blackerby purred, leaning close to Parry. "Very wise. This is dangerous information. But I cannot stop a threat I do not understand."

"The book doesn't say," Eliza said quickly.

"So, Shaw wanted this information either to control a dragon or to kill one." Westing frowned and stared at the broken window.

"Both," Phoebe said with a shudder. "He told me he would have liked to have a dragon or marry someone dragon-linked, but he ultimately wanted to rid England of dragons. I think he would take advantage of their power, but he wants to eliminate what he sees as an unfairness."

Blackerby shuddered dramatically. "We have another Cromwell on our hands. Or a Napoleon."

Eliza sighed to herself. She had seen enough unfairness in the West Indies to understand the desire to eliminate it, with wealthy plantation masters and the dragon-linked elite becoming ever more powerful off the labor of the less fortunate. But the problems seemed too big for one person to tackle, so while it troubled her, she didn't know how to change it. She chose to escape instead. She didn't want to see blood spilled over it, though. War brought hardship and famine more especially to the poor.

Blackerby extended a hand, and Eliza gladly passed the book to him, wiping her hand on her dressing gown. The Secretary of the

Home Office quickly scanned the pages, his eyes lighting with excitement.

"Indeed! The method is not entirely clear, but it sounds like they inadvertently killed the beast. It can be done. Astonishing."

Joshua frowned. "I thought St. George killed a wild dragon."

"A legend," Blackerby said. "We cannot be sure of the details. Some people say it was a dragon whose magic was corrupt and therefore no longer shielded him. Others say it was not a dragon at all, but a leviathan or some other creature without the magic dragons have for protection. Either way, this journal is the only documented story we have of a dragon dying."

"And Shaw was trying to find it," Westing said. "He knows it can be done, and now he wants to know how."

"Then we have to be sure to stop him." Blackerby scanned the pages. "Luckily, the book doesn't say exactly what they did. The knowledge may have been lost to history."

"That won't stop him from trying to recreate it," Phoebe said with a curl of her lips.

Eliza nodded. As long as Shaw was out there, they could not be safe.

"Does this mean there's not a dragon in the tor anymore?" Joshua's eyes widened, pleading.

Westing looked unsure how to answer, but Eliza rescued him. "I believe there is one. Our young dragons seem very interested in the tor, as if they know something is sleeping under it."

Blackerby twirled his quizzing glass. "If it's not the dragon whose skeleton that girl uncovered, there might still be some connection between the two. They were in close proximity."

"How does that help us?" Westing asked.

"We could try to communicate with it."

Westing clearly wanted to argue, but he let out an exasperated sigh and threw his hands up in surrender. "I doubt it will work, but there's no reason not to make the attempt."

Blackerby smiled. "Then I propose an excursion."

Chapter Fourteen

THEY WALKED the relatively short distance to the tor. Westing led the way, and Phoebe fell behind, her face pale and thoughtful.

Eliza slowed her pace to match Phoebe's. "Are you well?"

Phoebe tried to smile but only succeeded in grimacing. "I'm worried about Max."

"He probably snuck off to find a place to nap. I was tempted myself."

"Possibly." Phoebe shook her head. "It's more than that, though. Max and I have always been best friends, but since I met Westing, well, everything is different. I'm not even sure how Max is spending his time. Has he fallen into gambling? Is he in trouble?" Phoebe gestured helplessly. "I suppose things are meant to change as we grow older, but I had always thought Max and I would stay friends."

"I'm sure you're still friends," Eliza said. "Your relationship would have to be different, though, as you have new interests now."

"It might just be that, but I'm still worried about him. I wish he would talk to me about whatever is troubling him."

Eliza struggled to think of what she could say to comfort her friend on that score. Max's behavior did seem erratic, and getting more so on a regular basis.

"Sometimes, maybe we just have to trust people. You know Max isn't a fool. He'll come through all right."

Phoebe looked a little comforted by that idea, but what a hypocrite Eliza felt saying it. Whom did she really trust, after all? It had always seemed that everyone around her wanted something from her. Wanted to control her for their own ends. Oh, not Phoebe. Phoebe's sweet sincerity was why Eliza valued her friendship so much, but it also meant that Phoebe didn't really understand Eliza. That left Eliza with no one to turn to. To confide in. It was a heavy burden to carry her worries with no one to share them, and she grew weary of it.

The dragon tor rose before them, imposing in height compared to the surrounding hills rolling like the swells of gentle waves on a calm sea. They all stopped and craned their necks to see the top. Blackerby's dragon launched from his shoulder to circle above, but returned a few moments later making an unhappy clacking noise.

"What do you suppose was this dragon's connection was to the dead one?" Parry asked.

"We don't have evidence that dragons hibernate in pairs, even if they are mates," Blackerby said. "It may be that this dragon moved in when the other one was killed."

"It would not be very old then, for a dragon," Phoebe said.

Westing frowned up at the rocks and grass of the tor. "I'm still not convinced there's a dragon here anymore."

Eliza shifted. "I believe there is one. I feel like I can... sense it. I think Amethyst can, too."

"Mushroom has never reacted to it," Phoebe said. "Nor has Dragon."

Westing shook his head.

Blackerby toyed with his quizzing glass. "Perhaps, then, this dragon is a water dragon, giving Miss Prescott a certain sympathy with it. This resting place is close to the sea. I would very much like to confirm that this dragon is secure. I don't suppose you can communicate with the creature, Miss Prescott?"

"I wouldn't know how."

Blackerby looked to Westing. "Do you know of an entrance to the dragon's lair? You are all propriety now, but I'd wager you were an adventurous lad and ran wild around your estate."

Westing's mouth twitched. "Of course, as a boy I climbed all over the tor. I would have seen if there was a way in, but I never found one. It is full of nooks and crannies, though. Almost as if it collapsed at one point. So, we might find something if we dig."

"If only we had someone attuned to earth," Phoebe said. "They might be able to shift it."

Blackerby shook his head. "That is a dangerous ability. We would not want to inadvertently crush the dragon. It might not kill it, but it would not make us its friend."

"If we go looking for it, we may only alert Shaw to its presence," Parry warned.

"Everyone knows the dragon is there, don't they?" Eliza asked.

Westing nodded. "Shaw no doubt knows about it already."

"Is there any harm in trying to find the dragon, then?" Phoebe asked.

Westing shrugged. "Perhaps not."

The group drifted apart. The others crept around the tor, examining it for hidden entrances or clues about the dragon within. But Eliza stopped to listen. She sensed the dragon's restless presence. Its thoughts brushed over her mind, too faint to catch, smoke on the wind. They weren't clear or coherent, more like the mumbled fragments of someone talking in their sleep. A deep sense of unease washed over Eliza. A feeling that she was trapped and could not flee an unknown danger she sensed coming closer.

She shook her head and glanced up to see Parry watching her, her eyes concerned. She turned her back on him and wandered around the rise.

Eliza paused in her search, reaching out. Sensing. It seemed to her that there was something calling to her. Water. Maybe an underground pool or stream. She followed the sense of it, trying to find where the water might enter or exit the cavern beneath.

The sensation drew her to a little sunken area where some rocks had fallen in. She couldn't fit through any of the crevices—not even a tiny child could—but she could dig away some of the loose rocks. The water feeling drew closer, and she kept expecting to pull a handful of mud or damp stones from the ground, but all remained dry. She frowned, studying the opening, as bits of dirt slowly rolled in to fill the opening she had created.

Find it. Find it.

Eliza frowned and dug harder, trying to get some sense of what was under the dirt. Her fingers brushed something that gave her a start as if she had plunged them into icy cold water.

She yanked her hand back. Her fingers were dry.

She prodded the ground again, more carefully. There was something there. She couldn't see it, but it was smooth under her touch. She scrambled for it, and Amethyst hopped down to help her dig. The dragon scratched with a talon and pulled out a little piece of jewelry, dropping it at her knees and looking pleased with herself.

Eliza stared at it. A pearl brooch. Nothing very large or elaborate, and well-tarnished with age and dirt. But it sang of many waters. Eliza could feel the ocean's breeze and the rocking swell of waves beneath the deck of a ship as she stared at the little object. She wrapped the brooch in her fingers. It was like she had drawn the deep waters of the ocean up and sucked them inside of her. She rode with the waves, saw dolphins jumping in the wake of a ship and whisked past ancient behemoths of the deep that slept with one wary eye on the human world in the sun above. She gasped and dropped the brooch in her reticule.

The sensations faded.

It must have been the presence of the dragon—a water dragon—that let her see everything so clearly. This brooch could be part of its hoard. She wondered if she ought to leave it, but it had seemed to call to her. Perhaps the dragon wanted her to have it.

She looked up to see Parry watching her again, his expression curious. Eliza stood and brushed off her dress, giving him a challenging look. He said nothing, and Eliza didn't try to enlighten him. What would he understand about dragon magic? As Blackerby had said, her connection with the water dragon set her apart. And alone.

Finally, Blackerby called an end to the search.

"Well, my dears," he said, "At least if we can't find it, neither can our troublesome friend Shaw."

They trekked back to Westing Hall, none of them in a lively mood. Eliza followed Westing and Phoebe as they made their way toward the library, where laborers had boarded over the broken window.

Phoebe stepped into the library and gasped. "Max! What have you done?"

Eliza blinked, letting her eyes adjust to the dimness of the boarded-up room after the brilliance of the sun outside. Max stood in the library, and Deborah Shaw stood just behind him, as though hiding. The others crowded in alongside Eliza.

Max lifted his chin. "Maybe you're not the only one who can have ideas."

"What was your idea?" Westing snapped. "Kidnapping?"

Deborah flung herself in front of Max. "He did not kidnap me! I ran away all by myself!" She sounded extraordinarily pleased with herself.

"I have no doubt you did," Blackerby said, his mouth twitching with a smile. "But how did you find yourself in Mr. Hart's care?"

"I knew he wouldn't turn me in," Deborah turned worshipful eyes on Max. "And he didn't. Only, he convinced me I should reveal myself. For my own safety. He is so noble."

Max flushed, and Phoebe looked torn between amusement and exasperation.

"You've been hiding here?" she asked.

"In one of the ruins by the cliffs," Deborah said. "Max brought me food and made sure I was warm. I am sorry to have deceived you, Miss... Lady Westing. But it was *such* an adventure!"

"Heroics aside, what is your plan, both of you?" Westing sounded tired.

Max and Deborah shared a look. Deborah was the one who spoke. "I did not feel safe. Not knowing my uncle was out there. My aunt was very careless. I wanted to be somewhere where someone would watch over me."

Blackerby smirked. "Yet we believe your uncle is here."

"Here!" Deborah glanced around as though Shaw might be hiding in the bookshelves. "Has he followed me?"

"We did not suppose so," Blackerby said, "but now I cannot be sure. You have caused a great deal of trouble."

Deborah burst into tears.

"Now look what you've done!" Max exclaimed at Blackerby like a cockerel facing down a bemused mastiff.

Blackerby smiled. "Calm yourself, Mr. Hart. Miss Shaw has caused trouble, but I am not one who thinks that trouble is always bad."

Deborah sniffed and looked up.

"At least," Blackerby said, "We can keep a close eye on you here. And perhaps your knowledge of your uncle's past activities can be useful."

"Oh, yes, my lord. I can be very useful. Only, I don't know much at all."

Blackerby's mouth twitched again. "Well, Miss Shaw, we will do the best we can with you."

Chapter Fifteen

ELIZA WAS happy that at least part of Phoebe's unease about Max had been resolved. Still, she could sense the lingering rift between brother and sister. Was everyone destined to drift apart? Like the tides of the sea, time would bear them away. It filled her with an almost desperate longing for something stable and secure. And the house was beginning to feel rather crowded, with Blackerby striding about trailing shadows behind him like seaweed and Deborah's excited conversations dominating meals.

Seeking some solitary time the next morning, Eliza walked out toward the sea and stood where the cliffs splayed out toward the beach like the reaching talons of a dragon. As always, the water pulled at her, wanting to control her like everyone else did. Its call felt different this time, though. The cry of a lonely gull gliding on the wind. A never-ending search for something she couldn't name, a need to be always moving. She understood.

The pearl brooch weighed heavily in her reticule. She drew it out and pinned it to her bodice. Everything around her felt sharper: the crash of the waves against the rocks, the heaving of the ships gliding toward the bay, the scent of salt riding on the wind.

She touched the brooch. "What do you think, Amethyst? The

dragon seemed to want me to have this, and I'm sure her magic has touched it. But why?"

She felt stronger wearing it, like it was a token of good luck. And perhaps it would be. She returned to the house in a lighter mood that even Parry's speculative gaze couldn't spoil.

The reminder that they had Lady Sophie's dinner party to attend only dampened her mood a little. The brooch made her feel above Lady Sophie's supercilious remarks and equal to handling Randolph Blanchfield's leers.

Westing's party arrived at Lady Sophie's house for the dinner party just as it grew dark. Silhouetted figures moved in the windows of the grand house, illuminated by many candles. It reminded Eliza of her father's house in Dominica, but instead of homesickness, the sight filled her with dread. She touched the brooch, which she had added to her gown at the last moment, and drew her courage together to allow Westing to hand her down from the carriage.

Normally, she would be grateful for the distraction of a dinner party, but in the darkness beyond the house, she imagined Shaw and his agents watching. And when they stepped into the entrance hall, the servants hopped around them like seagulls looking for a bit of juicy gossip to snack on.

Eliza kept her chin up and pretended not to notice or care. Of course, people would have heard about the break-in at Westing Hall and be curious about it, especially with the murder of a local boy still unsolved.

Westing exchanged a few casual words with Lady Sophie in front of the butler and a footman, dropping a hint that the motivation for the break-in appeared to be a prank gone wrong by an old college associate.

Eliza nodded her approval. That would spread like fire and reassure people. No need to have the village in an uproar, especially not when Lyme needed autumn visitors and the money they spent in the village. The murder of the local boy was tragic, but most would reason that he must have been involved in something insidious. By telling themselves that—by blaming the dead—they could reassure themselves that they would never do anything so foolish. They could shield themselves with a false sense of security against a threat they could not fight anyway.

Eliza was relieved that the curiosity ebbed quickly. Lady Sophie, however, seemed to relish the gossipy chatter. She even stopped to whisper with an eager looking servant girl, probably one who often shared in the communications of the noble lady's loose tongue and enjoyed the prestige the high-born gossip gave her among her peers in the scullery.

Lady Sophie's party did not look any more cheerful than they had when Eliza had last seen them. Lady Millicent sulked over a book, Lady Amelia worked on a piece of embroidery with a stoic expression, and Mr. Hackett and Randolph Blanchfield lounged in a corner, looking bored as they passed a snuff box back and forth.

Pierre Moreau bounced up from the sofa. "Ladies! And gentlemen." He bowed quickly to Westing and Parry, but turned his attention back to Phoebe and Eliza, seizing and kissing both of their hands. "I am so delighted to see you also at tonight's dinner soiree. The more the merrier you say, yes?"

"Uh, yes," Phoebe agreed, looking like she was trying not to laugh.

Since Max had claimed he needed to watch over Deborah, Lady Zoe, and Westing's half-siblings, and Blackerby had shuddered and flatly refused to return to Lady Sophie's house, Eliza guessed that Moreau was there to even out the numbers and liven up the dreary house party. At least the Frenchman looked to be in a more jovial mood than her ladyship's regular guests.

The butler announced dinner, and they paraded into the dining room. Eliza ended up at the lower end of the table with Mr. Hackett. Lady Amelia and Moreau separated them from the rest of the party. Eliza resigned herself to a rather empty-headed dinner conversation. Everyone sat in a stiff tableau of uncomfortable politeness. Conversation revolved around the weather, the poor state of the roads, and, of course, hunting. From the snatches of conversation Eliza picked up at the other end of the table, they had settled into a pattern of delicate unfriendliness. Maybe talk of hunting wasn't so terrible.

Then, Lady Millicent said loudly, "Well, I came into town to do some shopping, and I could not believe how everyone chattered. I think rumors fly faster in small towns than in large ones, don't you?"

"Rumors?" Moreau asked, twitching his fork nervously. "What kind of rumors?"

"Oh, everyone seems to think there is some grand conspiracy going on full of murderers and revolution."

Moreau said nothing and did not seem to know where to look.

Lord Blanchfield yawned. "You should not listen to such foolish gossip, sister. They're probably only saying it to give the guests something to talk about besides the weather."

"Speaking of," Mr. Hackett said, "did you mention tomorrow will be a good day for riding? I'm itching to try my new animal on some of those jumps you pointed out to me."

"All this fuss about nothing," Lady Sophie said.

"Oh, but it's not nothing, is it Amelia?" Lady Millicent said. "What were they saying in the village, dear? It was quite shocking."

Amelia looked hesitant to speak. She poked at the meat with her fork, but her pale, freckled cheeks colored.

"Come, Amelia, you always remember details better than I do," Lady Millicent said.

Amelia looked up, resignation in her eyes. "They say there are dragon bones in the cliffs." Her glance swept toward Phoebe and Westing, and Eliza would have sworn she looked apologetic. Interesting.

Several of the guests gasped.

"Yes, that was it!" Millicent said, her eyes sparkling with the thrill of fresh gossip.

"But," Moreau said, "this is not possible. Dragons do not die."

"It's only a rumor," Amelia said quickly.

Lady Sophie waved a hand. "Oh, is that what the uproar is about? It's probably the old dragon they killed during the civil war."

Everyone went quiet and stared at her.

"What do you mean, Lady Sophie?" Westing asked.

"Your father knew the story. Didn't bother to tell you, did he? How strange, you being the dragon-linked in your family."

"I'm sure I don't know what you mean." Westing said slowly, each word measured.

"Then I am happy to tell you. I found the story in an old journal. It was from one of the earlier Lord Westings. They left all kinds of relics behind when they moved to Westing Hall."

"But the story?" Moreau prompted.

Lady Sophie waved her napkin. "Some of our forebearers killed a dragon during the Civil War. But not with weapons. With a little piece of treasure."

"How could a piece of treasure hurt anything?" Hackett asked.

"Oh, something about a mystical connection with the dragon's hoard." Lady Sophie picked up her fork. "It was all hushed up."

Eliza sat very still. This was another key to the mystery of the dragon bones. Shaw could never know or Britain was in serious danger.

And Eliza couldn't help think of the little piece of treasure she had found. That she wore on her bodice in front of everyone. She resisted the urge to touch it. To draw attention to it. But she felt Parry's gaze on her. She refused to look at him.

When they returned home, she sought the refuge of her room and pulled off the brooch, wrapping her fingers around it. Once again, it was like the sea itself flowed into her mind, and she nearly lost herself to it. So much power in her hands. Was this more than just a part of a dragon's hoard? Did it have some connection to the dragon that could be used against it? Maybe, then, the dragon was counting on Eliza to keep it safe.

But did she tell the others? It felt almost unfaithful to the dragon. Like it had shared a secret with her. Besides, if no one knew except her, Shaw could never find out. She might even find a way to communicate with the dragon—warn it of the danger it was in. Just as, she suspected, the dragon had been trying to warn them.

Chapter Sixteen

ELIZA RETURNED to the old Westing diaries, hoping to find any more hints about the brooch's connection to the dragon. She had to become master of it before Shaw or anyone else had a chance to.

Unfortunately, Blackerby was forever haunting the library, so Eliza took the book to the drawing room to read without his running commentary to distract her. Phoebe and Lady Zoe were in the room, Phoebe writing letters and Lady Zoe sewing, but they were more palatable company. As long as Max kept Deborah distracted in the gardens.

Eliza was just getting comfortable with the old handwriting when Westing's voice broke her concentration.

"Of course, come into the drawing room. My wife will want to hear this as well."

Phoebe looked startled and put her letter aside.

Westing led Mrs. Anning into the room. The woman clasped her hands nervously and gawked at the high ceiling with its frolicking, bare-bottomed angels.

Westing noticed his stepmother and said, "Ah, Lady Zoe, may I present to you Mrs. Anning. Her daughter is the skilled fossil hunter of Lyme."

"Charmed," Lady Zoe said, sounding sincere.

"Yes, my lady," Mrs. Anning said, curtseying back and forth to both Lady Westings like a weathercock in a storm.

"What was it you needed to see me about?" Westing asked, drawing her attention back.

"I hate to bring this to you, my lord, but my Mary has gone missing again. It might seem hard to believe, but this isn't like her, and I'm afraid she may have run into trouble."

Westing frowned. "I believe you. That does sound troubling. Have you told the constable?"

"No, my lord. On account of her dragon, and her not knowing who she could trust."

"Very well. We'll head to town to take up the search."

"Thank you, my lord!"

Baxter showed Mrs. Anning out, and Westing stared out the window for a few moments, looking his most intimidating. Then he peered out into the corridor.

"Jamie!" he called.

The boy galloped up to the drawing room and saluted.

"Impudent child," Westing growled, though he was smiling. "We're going into Lyme. Mary Anning has gone missing again, and I'm concerned. Shaw may be behind this. I want your ears to the ground."

"What both o' them, sir? I won't know which way to turn my 'ead."

Westing rolled his eyes. "Go on, urchin. This is serious."

Jamie scurried off, and Phoebe and Eliza went downstairs to the library to round up Blackerby.

"We'll leave Max to watch the house," Westing said. "He'll want to keep an eye on Miss Shaw anyway."

Phoebe nodded, her expression resigned. Brother and sister parted again.

Parry had been strolling the grounds—more like patrolling, Eliza thought—and he was anxious to join them.

"Phoebe, do you feel confident driving the phaeton to town?" Westing asked. "I want to ride ahead."

Phoebe hesitated, but Parry stepped up. "I'll drive the ladies. You and Blackerby ride."

Westing nodded. Eliza bristled a little that they had not bothered asking her, as she was quite capable of driving such a docile a pair as Westing kept for his phaeton, but it was no time to argue, with Mary possibly in danger.

She climbed into the phaeton with Phoebe and Jamie, and Parry—to his credit—made such good time that when they reached the Royal Lion, the grooms were still rubbing down the horses Blackerby and Westing had ridden.

They hurried out to the street, and Eliza spotted Lady Amelia coming out of the Royal Lion with a post-delivered packet clutched to her chest. She saw them, too, and tightened her grip on her parcel without acknowledging them. Eliza thought Lady Amelia was going to cut them completely, but she timed her steps so her path would cross theirs.

When she came close to Phoebe, she whispered, "Watch out for Lady Sophie."

Then she hurried on her way. Phoebe and Eliza shared a confused look, then Eliza shook her head. Lady Amelia was an odd girl.

Westing and Blackerby strode up the road toward them, presenting an odd contrast between Blackerby's tall, lean figure cloaked in shadows, and Westing's broad shoulders and white-blond hair.

Phoebe rushed forward to meet her husband. "Have you found them?"

He shook his head. "Blackerby has called for his yacht to be prepared so some of us can search by sea. Jamie, you'll see what you hear among the fishermen and servants, and you ladies can search the shore again. Perhaps Captain Parry will accompany you. You three had the best luck last time."

Parry nodded his agreement, but Eliza saw through Westing's plan: he was hoping to catch Shaw and didn't want the ladies in the way.

"Lord Westing!" Lady Sophie's sharp voice called from the doorway of the Royal Lion and rebounded off the neighboring buildings.

Phoebe's eyes widened, but there was no escape. The lady broke on them like a storm.

"There has been an outrage!" she announced, pounding her cane on the cobbled street.

Blackerby raised his quizzing glass to study the incensed lady. "Another one? There seems to be an outbreak."

Lady Sophie stood to her full height—barely more than half that of Blackerby's—and said, "Sir, this time, there has been an outrage against me."

His lips twitched in an obvious effort not to laugh. "Well, that is something. What is the nature of this outrage? An attempt on your person?"

She snorted derisively. "Don't make yourself an absurdity. It was a robbery. Someone broke into my library!"

Blackerby's smile faded, and Westing's attention fixed on her. "Your library? Did they take anything?"

"Of course! That's why it's a robbery!"

"What did they take?" Blackerby swung his quizzing glass on its chain, but the tightness in his voice belied his appearance of calm.

"I cannot yet be certain. The library was badly damaged, but many of my old books are now missing."

"The Westing journals?" Westing asked, his tone flat.

"Possibly," she said dismissively. "Among others. Some of those old editions are very valuable."

Westing rubbed his eyes. "Have you told the constable?"

"I have told you—the local lord is better than some bumbling constable. You will see that the villain responsible is brought to justice."

"Of course, I will look into this. Immediately. Do you have a safe place to stay?"

"I have brought my party to the Royal Lion for now, though I'm certain Westing Hall would be more comfortable for me."

Eliza groaned inwardly. Maybe *she* would take a room at the Royal Lion. An inn would be less crowded than Westing Hall at this point.

Westing sighed. "I have rooms available, but you should know that there was a break-in at my house as well."

"What!" Lady Sophie looked like a ruffled hen. "Is nothing sacred? I shall remove myself to London. I hate the city, but at least there we are safe from these… these…."

"Outrages?" Blackerby supplied.

Lady Sophie glared at him. "Indeed. And aren't you supposed to do something about them, Lord Secretary?"

"Indeed, my lady, and I shall."

"Very well. I remove myself to London. My cousins and their friends will have to stay elsewhere. For your sakes, I hope they make themselves comfortable at the Royal Lion rather than descending upon you."

They bowed their farewell to her. No one spoke until she was safely out of earshot.

Blackerby let his quizzing glass drop and spin at the end of its ribbon. "So, we have a spy in our midst."

Phoebe gave a start. "You think so?"

"Of course," Westing said. "Someone who was at that dinner alerted Shaw to the existence of the other Westing diaries, and Shaw now knows at least as much as we do about how to hurt the dragon."

"Perhaps more," Blackerby said. "Because Mary Anning is missing, and if Shaw was bold enough to take her, he must have had a reason. He thinks she can help him find whatever he needs to kill or control dragons."

Eliza quailed with guilt at that. She didn't know how the brooch related to the dragon, but she suspected it might be what Shaw was searching for. Was it her fault that Mary had been kidnapped? But no, Shaw could not know of the brooch. And that meant neither could the spy, whether that was one of Lady Sophie's guests or even one of her servants. Perhaps Lady Sophie herself. Eliza could not afford to trust anyone.

She felt Captain Parry's gaze on her, but she ignored him. Whatever he might guess, and however he guessed it, she would not confirm his suspicions.

Westing and Blackerby hurried back for the port, Jamie scurried away, and Parry turned to study Phoebe and Eliza.

"Which way do we search, loves?"

"East, where we found the landslide," Phoebe said.

Eliza nodded. "The dragon bones are at the heart of this mystery."

Parry looked to the east, and the wind brushed his sun-bleached hair back. "Sounds reasonable. Let's be off."

They did not travel far before they encountered another landslide. The mud and boulders slid down across their path and into the water, completely blocking their way.

"It's not natural," Eliza said.

"No." Parry paced over to study it. "If anything, this confirms what we suspected. Shaw may have set this off to cover his tracks. We'll have to find a way around it. Lady Westing, see if your husband has sailed. If not, the yacht is our best hope. I'll see if I can find a local fishing boat, in case." He hesitated, looking to Eliza.

"I'll be fine waiting here," she said. "Amethyst will protect me."

He nodded and strode away. Phoebe sent Mushroom flying ahead of her, half-running along the promenade toward the bay.

Eliza turned back to study the landslide. Had Shaw forced Mary to bring down the cliffside and block their path? She touched the brooch in her reticule, running her fingers over the silky-smooth pearls. When she did, the sound of the waves rushed around her. She felt the frustration and anger of the sea at finding the landslide blocking its way, the power of the tides pressing on the offending soil in the water's domain.

The sea wanted to be rid of the landslide, and a stirring of magic starting in Eliza's chest and tingling down to the tips of her fingers suggested that she could help it.

Eliza extended her hand, and the waves surged forward, slamming against the landslide and dragging mud and boulders into the water to be scattered. A stinging rush of energy flowed over her like a wave then receded, leaving her trembling. This was unlike any magic she had experienced or even heard of. If she had the strength to do the same several times, she might clear away the landslide, but it had left her exhausted. Perhaps this power was meant for dragons, not humans.

But when she looked to Amethyst, her dragon was playing in the surf, uninterested in her activities. Eliza lost herself in watching the rhythmic dance of the waves.

"Beautiful, isn't it?"

Eliza jumped and turned to face Parry. "What was that?"

He glanced at the sea, but then his gaze returned to her. "Beautiful. So near, and yet so unholdable." He looked out past the landslide to the water, his eyes alight with bittersweet memories. "That was something I learned early: We who sail the ocean must love her, but we can never keep her."

"Hmm." Eliza said. Was he trying to tell her the brooch wasn't hers to keep? But he went on.

"I cannot imagine what it must be like to have even a drop of the sea's power. Overwhelming, I suppose. I see you wrestling with your water magic."

Eliza wanted to snap at him that it was none of his concern, but it felt so good to be understood for once. She turned to face Parry. "The sea took my mother, you know."

He nodded once.

She took a deep breath. "I have always wished I could control it. That I could make it so it can't hurt anymore. But I can't. It's too much." Even with the brooch's power, she knew this was true. "I've often wished I was attuned to something else."

Parry smiled sadly. "I know, love. And I'm sorry it causes you pain. There is beauty in its wildness, though. Its unpredictability. It can be fierce, but those unexpected moments like St. Elmo's fire dancing on the mast, the sun setting over the endless horizon, the gentle rocking of the waves like a cradle. I suppose they're sweeter because of the danger. The pain."

Eliza scowled and looked away. "Perhaps."

"One thing I know," Parry said gently, "Is that you can't hold on to it. You can't fight the tide. You have to ride it."

Eliza gave him a sour look and didn't reply. What could she say? Parry was probably right, but that didn't help her much.

She looked away from the sea, scanning the beach. In the bay, ladies climbed into colorful rolling boxes that local girls guided into the water so the ladies could bath in privacy. The local girls also kept the ladies from panicking and going under. Eliza's first reaction was to scoff at the silly women, but then she realized maybe they were wise to be nervous.

A little girl wandered among the bathers, offered colorful sea-polished pebbles in a basket.

Eliza felt in her reticule, but she had finally spent through her pin money. She grimaced and turned to Parry.

"Will you advance me a few pence? I want to buy some rocks."

The warm look left Parry's face. "At a time like this?"

"There is nothing to do at this moment but wait anyway."

"And waste your time on fripperies?"

Eliza dug her nails into her palm. "They may seem like fripperies to you, with your ships and your wars, but what else do I have? I don't have a man's resources or freedom to help search for poor Mary Anning. I can't fight. I wasn't even allowed to drive myself into Lyme. So, yes, while I wait on the men to decide what's best, I will do one of the few things I do have control over and spend my money on something that makes me happy, and makes certain that little girl's family eats tonight, too!"

Parry looked taken back by this. "You feel that trapped?"

"Of course! Have you not been paying attention? You men are all alike! You, my father, all of you think so little of women that you forget that we might have our own hopes and desires outside of anything you might scheme."

Parry studied her, his face dark. Eliza partly regretted offending him, but she was so weary of always having to put on a pretty smile to keep the men around her happy. If she couldn't have any other freedom, at least she might be allowed to say what she really felt.

Parry pulled a heavy coin purse from his pocket and held it out to Eliza.

"I don't need all your money," she said, now feeling more guilty.

"This is yours," Parry said. "I cannot help you with any of the rest of it, but I'll give you what you've been asking for: you are free of me. I won't try to hold you. Just tell me when you need more money, and you'll have it."

He walked away. Eliza quickly hid the coin purse in her reticule then stared after him in shock. She should have been elated, but she only felt a hollow numbness and a strange tightness in her throat.

Phoebe hurried back over the beach, her cheeks flushed.

"Captain Parry!" she called.

He turned, his face unreadable as he squinted into the wind.

She motioned him west to the port. "They're waiting on the tide, but it is turning. Blackerby will watch for you, but you must hurry!"

He tipped his hat to her and walked away at a fast clip, not looking back.

Phoebe caught up with Eliza, pausing for a moment to catch her breath. Then she glanced at Eliza's face.

"What's wrong?" Phoebe asked.

"Oh, Captain Parry is just being… himself!"

Phoebe smiled a little. "Handsome and charming?"

"Perhaps those things, too," Eliza growled. "But he is so difficult. Mystifying."

Phoebe put a gentle hand on Eliza's arm. "He always shows a great deal of concern for you. I think he cares for you deeply."

Eliza grew warm and then cold at the thought. "If so, he has an odd way of showing it. But… perhaps."

"It must be complicated for him. He is supposed to be your trustee. Your guardian. He has to behave with the utmost propriety. Anything else would be scandalous."

"It would be a disaster," Eliza said.

Phoebe looked perplexed. Eliza shook her head. How could she make Phoebe understand? If she couldn't convince her friend, she wasn't sure she could convince herself, either.

"Don't you see?" Eliza said. "I need him to keep his distance. I could never be free with Captain Parry because…. because I think I could love him."

Phoebe's eyes widened. "But—Isn't that good?"

"No. Because if I loved him, I would not be in control of anything anymore. I would be in his power."

"I suppose love does make us vulnerable," Phoebe said thoughtfully. "I don't think he would abuse that power, though. And as long as he loved you in return…"

Eliza squeezed her eyes shut, willing away the tears that threatened to form. "I would always be waiting for the day when I lose him. Like I lost my mother. And, it's that much worse that he loves the sea. It's the thing that took my mother from me. I cannot let it take anything else from me."

Phoebe squeezed Eliza's arm. "I can see why you're afraid. But wouldn't it be better to take the chance of having some happiness rather than condemning yourself to knowing you'll be trapped in a loveless marriage?"

The word 'trapped' stung Eliza. She wouldn't really be trapped if she married someone like Randolph Blanchfield, because he wouldn't care what she did. But she would be giving up any chance at ever choosing love. Every choice led to some consequence, and that meant she was trapped no matter what she chose—or if she chose nothing at all. Even that was also a choice. Eventually, Randolph Blanchfield and Captain Parry and everyone else would move on, and she would be left alone. Was that freedom?

Eliza smiled weakly at her friend. "For now, let's concern ourselves with Mary Anning. Maybe we can hear some useful gossip around town. Or at least be of some use to her mother. Oh, but before we go, I wanted to buy some of the colorful rocks that child is selling."

Phoebe nodded, and if she didn't perfectly understand, she at least showed sympathy for Eliza's confusion.

Chapter Seventeen

BLACKERBY'S YACHT WAS A SLEEK, Bermuda-rigged sloop, its tall, triangular sails taut in the wind, ready to spring forward. She would be a fast one. Parry was happy to step onto the deck of a ship again. The rocking of the waves was familiar, his home since he was fourteen. Here, he understood what was expected of him.

Much different than dealing with Eliza Prescott. He didn't know what to do about the empty ache inside him when he thought of her, but he did know one thing: it was not his place to keep a hold on her, any more than he could hold back the tides.

His place, for now, was to find Mary Anning.

Westing looked much less happy to be putting out to sea. His face betrayed little, but his jaw was tightly clenched, and he fought against the rocking of the ship.

"I'm surprised you don't have a yacht," Parry said. "Living so close to the sea."

Westing grimaced. "Father's cutter took him and my brother to the bottom of the channel."

Parry winced, but Blackerby cut in. "Luckily, I came prepared."

"Can you sense which way they went?" Westing asked Blackerby.

Parry cocked an eyebrow, but Blackerby shook his head. "As before, Shaw leaves no trace of emotion. Like he doesn't have any."

Parry had seen men like that while sailing. Those who had lost all human feeling—or had never had it in the first place. They were effective in battle, but not safe in society.

"Jamie did find some fishermen who saw a girl who might have been Mary being roughly escorted by an older man this morning," Westing said. "Some of the lads chased him down, but he slipped away from them."

Parry's stomach felt icy as he imagined a child in the hands of an evil man like Shaw. "The landslide to the east seems like our best lead." He told them what he had seen.

"Then we go east," Blackerby said and gave the order to cast off.

Parry turned his face to the salty spray. Shaw had a head start on them, but they would travel faster. They slid past the landslide that had stopped his progress on the shore, a friendly wind hurrying them on their way. Luck was with them.

They approached the stretch of shoreline where Mary had shown them the dragon skeleton. Parry had his spyglass trained on the beach, and he saw two figures there, one small and the other full grown.

"I think I see them!" he called.

Blackerby swore. "The water is rocky here."

But the figures on shore were moving now. The adult—it was Shaw, Parry guessed—dragged the smaller figure toward the surf.

"He's got a boat," Parry reported. "A little rowboat. He's taking it between the rocks."

Blackerby was at his side, his own spyglass in hand. "He knows we can't follow him among the rocks. He may be making for a piece of land where he can run inland. If he reaches the open waters, we'll run him down." The man's grin was practically draconic, and the dark gray dragon on his shoulder flapped its wings and hissed.

The water rushed and foamed around the vessels, but Shaw expertly steered his little boat among the rocks. They were close enough that Parry could see Mary clearly now through the spyglass. She was looking between Shaw and the water. It would be foolhardy to jump in, but maybe she thought her chances better with the waves than with the madman.

Something was off, though. It took Parry a moment to realize what it was. The girl's dragon was nowhere to be seen. Dragons did not leave their humans. Not willingly. What had Shaw done?

Blackerby's shadows spread across the water like spilled ink, racing for the rowboat.

Mary looked toward the sloop.

"Don't do it," Parry whispered. "Stay in the boat."

She jumped overboard.

Parry swore, stripped off his coat, boots, and leg, and launched himself into the sea as Blackerby shouted a warning at him.

He hit the cold water with a gasp and struck out for the girl being tossed about by the waves. She slammed into a rock and managed to grab onto it as the current pushed and pulled her skirts. She would not be able to hold on long.

"Get Shaw!" Blackerby called from the deck of the sloop.

Parry looked to the boat and the man furiously rowing it, a hat pulled low to hide his face. This was Parry's chance to catch the villain. It was the right and patriotic thing to do. Shaw might have a gun, but using it would mean dropping the oars, and if Parry capsized the rowboat, the gun would do Shaw no good. Parry would have the man.

Parry treaded water and glanced back at Mary. She barely hung onto the rock. Strands of dark hair were plastered to her pale face, and she gasped for air as the waves pounded her.

"Shaw, man!" Blackerby cried. "Don't let him slip away!"

The current bore the rowboat farther from Parry. He growled to himself and turned his back on Shaw to rescue Mary Anning. Blackerby shouted something unintelligible and no doubt rude, but Parry ignored him. The sloop sailed on to cut Shaw off, but Parry didn't worry about that, either. He reached Mary Anning.

The waves thrashed both of them about. A scrape on Mary's cheek bled freely, and her hands were cut up, her lips blue with cold.

"Let go of the rock," Parry called. "Swim to me."

"Don't know if I can," Mary said, teeth chattering.

The sea dipped beneath Parry, and he touched bottom for a

moment. Then the next swell propelled him up and knocked Mary loose from her rock as well. Parry grabbed the girl as another trough threatened to dash them against the rock that had been her anchor. Parry managed to push off of it, swimming for the shore. He bore the brunt of a wave slamming them into another rock, but then the surf pushed them toward the pebble-strewn beach.

Mary found her footing and crawled forward while Parry dragged himself free of the grip of the sea, the taste of salt water in his mouth and nose, and his skin itchy with brine.

Mary sat there gasping and shivering for several minutes while Parry struggled to catch his breath.

"Are they coming back for us?" she asked, her teeth chattering.

"Westing will, anyway" Parry said, scanning the sea and regretting that he had to leave his spyglass on the sloop. And his leg. He liked that one; it fit better than most. Blackerby was probably vexed enough to drop them both into the water.

Parry scooted around to stare up at the cliff. Much more of the dragon's bones were exposed. He wanted to ask Mary about it, but when he looked over at her, she was quietly crying.

"There, now, lass," he said. "What's wrong?"

She sniffled and tried to wipe her tears away with the heels of her hands.

"He took Sandy!"

"Your dragon?" Parry asked. "Why?"

"To make me do what he said. He said he would hurt Sandy if I didn't help him. After seeing those dragon bones in the cliff, I was afraid. I didn't want to let him row me away somewhere far from my mum either, though. So, I decided to escape. I don't know if I've done right."

More tears trickled down her face.

"You were right to save yourself, lass," Parry said.

Mary rested her forehead on her drawn-up knees and said nothing.

"Ahoy!"

Parry started and turned to see Blackerby and Westing striding toward them, Blackerby wielding a cane over the rocky shore. Westing, bless him, had a bundle that looked like it included Parry's leg.

Blackerby's captain must have found a place where they could get to shore. And Shaw must have escaped.

"Shaw had a sailing ship waiting for him," Blackerby said with a dark look at Parry. "I thought my sloop was fast, but this one outraced us."

"At least we can find out what Shaw was after," Westing said quickly. "And I'm glad to see you safe, Miss Anning, Captain Parry."

Blackerby looked doubtful about the benefits of that development compared to Shaw's escaping. Parry regretted that the man had slipped through their fingers, but he could not regret saving a child's life.

Parry filled the other two men in on Mary's missing dragon while he strapped his leg back on.

"Can he kill my dragon?" Mary asked when Parry had finished.

Parry wished they could tell the girl that Shaw wouldn't be able to hurt the creature, but he was no longer so certain. "I don't think he can, dragon bones notwithstanding."

"Some of that depends on what happened here," Blackerby said, holding up his quizzing glass to study the exposed dragon bones.

"What did he want?" Westing asked Mary gently.

"He's insane. He wanted me to bring down the whole cliffside. He thinks there's a treasure inside it."

"An actual treasure?" Blackerby asked. "Like a dragon hoard?"

"That's what I thought he meant. I told him if there was piles of gold in the cliffside, everyone would know it by now. Some of it would have washed into the sea, and everyone would have gone mad digging it out. But he said it might just be one small treasure." She bit her lip. "And I think he's right."

"Why do you say that?" Blackerby asked.

"Because I can sense something in there. It's not big, but it also feels foreign. Not like the rock around it. It doesn't belong. It's almost like it's talking to me. In my head."

"Fascinating," Blackerby said. "Is it normal for you to sense anomalies under the soil?"

"If you mean where things are in the dirt, then yes. Not very deep, but if it's close to the top, it nags at my brain, like something out of place on a shelf. But it's never felt like it wanted to be found before."

"Hmm. And you can move soil as well?" Blackerby asked.

"A little. More like, I can pull at the things that don't belong."

Blackerby's eyes glittered with interest. "Very interesting. You see, you have the same attunement as our king and Prinny, errr... the Prince Regent, but it manifests in different ways."

She looked more confused than impressed by that news. "Is that why that man took my dragon?"

"He probably wanted it for leverage, hoping you'll find whatever treasure he's after and trade it for your dragon."

"Well, then I will. I want Sandy back."

"I'm afraid we can't let you do that," Blackerby said. "But we will do everything in our power to free... er, Sandy. In fact, I'm going to ask you to help us locate this treasure."

She crossed her arms. "How are you any better than him, then?"

"We are not trying to foment rebellion." Blackerby said.

Westing hurried to add, "We will get your dragon back whether you help us or not."

This softened her wary expression. "All right, then. It's deep, though. I'll show you where to dig, but you have to be careful you don't bring the cliff down on our heads. I can't stop mud once it starts sliding."

Parry had not expected this rescue mission to involve digging into the side of a cliff, but there he was, his hands coated with dirt as he tossed aside fossils and rocks in a search for some little trinket the girl sensed under the surface. He also pulled loose a dragon bone, stained brown instead of bleached white after its long rest under the surface. They were disturbing a grave, after all. Robbing it, even.

As he scraped away another layer of dirt, his fingers fumbled over something too smooth to be natural. He whisked away the rest of the soil to reveal something bronze. He dug it out and scraped away the clinging mud. A ring.

"Found something!" he called, brushing more dirt off. It was plain bronze with a stylized dragon etched on the bezel.

Westing and Blackerby, on either side of him, stopping their own scrambling in the dirt to look.

Parry held the ring out to Mary.

She took it and nodded. "Yes, that's it."

Blackerby held out a hand, and Mary reluctantly dropped the ring into it. The earl inspected it under his quizzing glass. "Interesting. It's very old. Roman, I'd say. But not particularly valuable. Are you certain this is what Shaw was looking for?"

Mary shrugged. "No. But it's the only thing like a treasure I sense in there with the dragon bones. The only thing that's not fossils, rocks, or other normal things. And I think it's the thing that's pulling at me like it wanted to be found."

"Then this may be what all of the fuss is about." Blackerby tossed the ring up and caught it, peering through the hole. "But why?"

Chapter Eighteen

WHEN ELIZA and Phoebe grew weary of traipsing up and down the promenade, hoping to somehow ferret out a clue about Shaw, they returned to the Royal Lion.

They found Jamie sitting in the common room, sipping tea with an air of propriety completely at odds with his dirty clothes and the wild hair poking out from under his cap. Eliza supposed the landlord must have seen him before, but the man still kept a wary eye on the boy.

She and Phoebe joined his table.

That brought a change of demeanor from the landlord, who hurried over to ask how he could serve them.

After they ordered their own tea and cakes, the landlord looked to Eliza.

"Begging your pardon, but you're Miss Elizabeth Prescott?"

"I am."

"There's a letter come for you, then."

He hurried to bring it over with their tea. Eliza checked the direction. It had been sent to her lodgings in London and then forwarded on to Lyme Regis. The handwriting looked like her father's. It must have been sent some months before, since she had written to her father to tell him she would be spending the autumn and winter months with the Westings. He would be delighted when he learned her host was a viscount.

She broke the seal and skimmed the contents. Each line struck her with increasing doubt and shock until she set the letter down and stared at it like it had transformed into an eel.

"Eliza?" Phoebe asked.

Eliza grimaced and ripped the paper, a satisfying *schick* under her fingers.

"My father is a… is a…"

"A fogram!" Jamie offered.

"Yes, a fogram!" Eliza said. She didn't know the cant word, but she liked the way it sounded. "And also a… a…"

Jamie's grin sparkled with mischief. "A lout. A thatch-gallows. A weasel-gutted bachelor's son!"

"Jamie!" Phoebe put a hand on the boy's arm. "I don't know what those words mean, but by the way people are looking at you, I'm certain you shouldn't be shouting them. Eliza, stop laughing. You're only encouraging him." Her expression softened. "What upset you?"

Eliza's merriment vanished. "Oh, this letter from my father." She waved the fragments. "Apparently, he *wants* me to marry Lord Randolph Blanchfield."

"Scaly clump," Jamie muttered.

"What?" Phoebe looked appalled.

"I called that cove a—"

"Hush, not you." Phoebe said to Jamie. She lowered her voice. "Eliza, you can't mean that your father knows Lord Blanchfield and still wishes for you to marry him?"

"He has heard that the man is an idiot and thinks him an ideal match. A stupid husband with good connections and a future in the House of Lords? Apparently, that is my father's idea of a darling husband. I thought…" Eliza balled the bits of torn letter. "I did not think he could care so little for me."

Phoebe put an arm around her shoulders, but Eliza barely felt her comforting touch. She was nothing more than a dress-up doll after all. A Bartholomew baby. Her future was just like her past, though a dandy husband would replace her dandy father lavishing her with fine gowns and expecting her to smile and be charming for his friends. Maybe there was nothing better awaiting her than Lord Randolph Blanchfield.

Eliza sipped her tea, not really tasting it, and stared out the window at the dismal gray sky hanging over Lyme. The storm moving in smelled of the sea, and an urge to stop it—to fight the constant pressure of the water's might—seized Eliza. She touched the brooch in her reticule. The roar of the sea rushed in her ears. She could take up the brooch and command the waves. She could toss the brooch in the depths of the sea and never think of it again. The weight of either was too great. She withdrew her hand and did nothing but try to make small conversation with Phoebe.

It seemed an age before the door swung open and the men entered, Mary Anning with them. The girl looked pale, but something flickered in her eyes that Eliza recognized: defiance.

Phoebe jumped to her feet. "You found her! Is she well? And what of Mr..." She glanced around the room and gave Westing a significant look.

He shook his head, and the faint flicker of hope Eliza had felt puffed out like a snuffed candle. She tried to meet Parry's gaze. The salt-crusted state of his clothes suggested he had been in the thick of the excitement. But he avoided looking her way. He had washed his hands of her, after all.

Blackerby strolled around the room, studying the assorted locals and travelers through his quizzing glass. "Perhaps we can continue this conversation at Westing Hall?"

The landlord looked disappointed to be missing out on both their patronage and their gossip, but they paid their shot and headed back to Westing Hall. The rain drizzled down on them before they reached its shelter, and everyone was forced to change clothes and reassemble in the drawing room. Max and Deborah joined them, Deborah all agog to hear the news about her uncle.

Mary Anning was there with them, too, in a clean but well-worn dress that had perhaps belonged once to a young housemaid.

"Miss Anning will be staying with us until Shaw is found," Westing said. "Her mother thought it would be safer."

"That man took my dragon," Mary said. "Lord Westing promised to get her back."

Eliza's eyes widened at the news and the rash promise. She wondered what Parry thought of this, what insights he had on their adventure, but he stared out the window at the rain tracing trickling gray paths along the glass.

"My uncle stole someone's dragon?" Deborah asked, teasing her own dragon with a piece of string. She looked at young Mary. "Hers?"

Phoebe looked to her husband in fear. "Why?"

"Because I wouldn't give him what he wanted," Mary said, watching Deborah through narrow eyes as though the young woman might be in league with Shaw.

"That's simple, then," Deborah said. "He'll send you a ransom. Trade the dragon for whatever it is he wants."

"Well reasoned, my dear Miss Shaw," Blackerby said. "But what if it would be dangerous to give in to him?"

"Oh," Deborah's expression fell. "I hadn't considered that."

"My poor Sandy." Mary's chin quivered, and she looked as though only stubbornness was keeping her from bursting into tears.

"He can't hurt the dragon, though," Deborah said, brightening again. "He's tried, and he won't waste time on something that doesn't work."

Mary did not look reassured at that.

Westing quickly turned his full attention to her. "Miss Anning, Lady Westing's maid will take you to your room and make sure you are comfortable. Let her know if you need anything."

Mary nodded, awe of the promised attention from a fine lady's maid distracting her momentarily.

"I think we should send Molly to keep her company," Phoebe said, referring to a pickpocket they had rescued from the streets and now employed in the kitchen.

"I defer to your judgement," Westing said with a smile and slight bow.

Once Mary was safely out of the room, Eliza studied the men's faces. "Tell us what happened."

Westing summarized their adventure.

"He only wanted a ring?" Eliza asked. "Just a single object from the dragon's hoard?"

"That doesn't sound like my uncle at all!" Deborah looked to Max, her eyes confused.

Blackerby twirled something in his fingers and held it up. "This ring, we believe. Roman. Not valuable on the surface, but I think he wanted to possess both the object and the information about it. It was the only treasure buried with the dragon, and Mary said it called to her somehow."

Eliza gave a start at that and quickly shifted positions in her chair to cover the sudden movement. Was this ring like her brooch?

"So, is it magic?" Phoebe asked.

Blackerby shrugged and tossed it to her. She caught it.

"Not that I can see," Blackerby said. "But how would we know? Unless someone wants to try to use it on their own dragon?"

Eliza, Deborah, Westing, and Phoebe all shook their heads.

"Anyway," Eliza said. "From what I've read in the journals, the item the men tried to use to control the dragon had some value to that particular creature."

Blackerby held out a hand, and Phoebe tossed the ring back to him. "But if it was the sentimental value of the ring that the dragon cared about, what good would it do Shaw? That dragon is bones and dust. No, there must be something more to it."

Blackerby tried the ring, slipping it onto one of his long, slender fingers. Everyone watched him with bated breath, though Eliza's hand slipped down to her reticule, her thoughts on the brooch there.

Blackerby shook his head. "Nothing, as far as I can tell. I sense no power from it, no extra connection to my dragon."

"What about a connection to the elements?" Eliza blurted out.

He tilted his head and looked to be concentrating. Finally, he grimaced and removed the ring. "No. And it's not even an attractive ring."

He wiped his hand on his coat and held the ring out disdainfully. They each tried wearing it. Eliza sensed nothing from the ring. It was smooth, cool, and a little loose on her finger. A dead thing, nothing like the brooch. They let each of their dragons examine it, and none seemed any more interested than they might be in another piece of jewelry, and not a very pretty one at that, as Blackerby said.

Phoebe watched Mushroom bat at the ring with bored indifference. "Mushroom likes bright, shiny things. I don't see why the ring would even appeal to him. Dragon, either. He likes things that remind him of ice, I think."

Eliza nodded. Her dragon paid almost no attention to the dirty thing. "Amethyst has always been more attracted to objects that came from water: shells, smooth pebbles, sometimes shiny jewels that glinted like the sun off the waves. Only Lord Blackerby's dragon seems even the slightest bit interested in this ring." She shuddered and decided not to speculate too much on why. His dragon must be drawn to dark and secretive things.

Max held the ring up to examine it. "Can't see why any but an earth dragon would want something that had been buried in dirt for hundreds of years."

"I wonder if it belonged to the dragon's human," Phoebe said. "It does seem to have been old enough."

"That's kind of sweet," Eliza said. "To think that dragons keep their baby hordes. Older dragons must be able to collect much more impressive items than the little trinkets we give them."

"Like an adult keeping a favorite childhood toy," Phoebe said. "I still have a doll from when I was little."

Eliza had left everything of her childhood behind when she came to England. Everything except a necklace of uneven pearls spaced on a silver chain that had been her mother's. That was too precious to leave, though it was not fine enough to wear on most occasions. She glanced at the bronze ring sitting in Max's palm. Precious because of the memories it carried.

"What is it Shaw told you about the connection between dragons and their human?" she asked Phoebe.

Phoebe screwed her eyes shut for a moment. "Oh, that it may be from us that dragons get their connection to their element. The magic comes from them, the element comes from their human."

"But once their human dies, they keep their connection to the element."

"Yes, I suppose they became bonded to it through their human."

"But what if they need something to maintain that bond?" Eliza pointed to the ring.

Blackerby plucked the ring from Max's palm. "Maybe. Maybe the ring would respond to someone attuned to earth. Like His Highness, our dear Prinny."

Phoebe's eyes widened. "Or like Mary Anning."

"Poor child!" Deborah groaned. "Her dragon isn't for ransom. He's setting a trap for her. Wicked man! I would purge his blood from my veins if I could."

Max put an arm around her shoulders. "There, now. We know his crimes are none of your doing."

She nodded but looked miserable.

Eliza touched the brooch through the fabric of the reticule, a heavy feeling growing in her stomach. What did that mean for her? What did the dragon expect her to do with this burden? "But the journals also said that they used the item against the dragon somehow."

Blackerby tucked the ring into a hidden waistcoat pocket. "Perhaps having a connection to an element also gives you a connection to the dragons attuned to it. Unless Miss Anning is inclined to experiment, Prinny may have to be the one to explore that theory." His lips curled slightly in distaste.

But Eliza felt no added connection to Amethyst. Shaw may have miscalculated. Or he only hoped to force Mary to use the ring's powers. Eliza could answer at least some of their questions, though. She had to tell them about the brooch. But she suddenly felt ashamed for having kept it a secret.

Baxter entered the room, and guilty relief flooded Eliza at his interruption.

"My lord," he said, holding out a silver tray with a set of visiting cards.

Westing took them with an expression of foreboding and groaned. "The Blanchfield party has paid us a visit."

"Shall I send them away, my lord?" Baxter asked.

"Give us a moment, Baxter."

With the butler out of the room, Parry finally contributed to the conversation. "One of them may well be a spy."

"They could have come for Mary," Phoebe said.

"I know," Westing said through clenched teeth. "Or to discover what we know."

"I like my enemies where I can see them," Blackerby said. "If we keep them distracted here, we might learn something, and we can send them away with misinformation."

Westing drew his lips back in a grimace. "We would have to keep all of this quiet. Nothing about Mary. Nothing about the ring or dragon bones. Keep conversation so shallow that no one can bring up any dangerous topics."

"Easily done!" Blackerby said.

Westing looked skeptical, but he poked his head out the door to instruct Baxter.

Eliza clenched her fists in her lap. She couldn't keep her thoughts shallow; her worries plunged too deep. Her confession would have to wait. For now, she had to decide what to do with Randolph Blanchfield's attentions. He might offer her more freedom than her father did. But it didn't seem like freedom when it made her stomach feel hard and sick.

Danger. Danger. Danger.

Eliza took a deep breath and squeezed her eyes shut, wishing she could talk back to the voice that whispered in her mind. *I don't know what to do.*

Chapter Nineteen

ELIZA HAD NEVER SEEN A MORE miserable dinner party, and she had plenty of experience in the matter. Westing's cook was probably cursing his name to the heavens, being asked to throw together an appropriate meal on such short notice. Deborah returned to hiding in the back rooms or gardens with Max to guard her. Blackerby smiled serenely at the awkward gathering, but he was perverse. Phoebe's smile looked more like a grimace as she tried to keep up a safe conversation with Lady Amelia. Westing did not hide his scowl at being forced to entertain Mr. Hackett and Lady Millicent, who seemed determined to flirt with every man in the room, even down to the footman.

Every man except her brother, of course, which left Lord Randolph Blanchfield to Eliza. She avoided him for a while by trying to join Phoebe's disjointed conversation with Lady Amelia, but eventually she found herself cornered.

Cornered. Yes, that was how she felt. Like a trapped animal seeking release from a cage. She had stepped into the snare she laid.

"I don't know why you're being coy," Lord Blanchfield said, taking her hand with a self-assured smile. "I think we both know that we can be an advantage to one another if we came to an arrangement."

Eliza wanted to tug her hand away, but she didn't, resigning herself to the conversation. "What would be the nature of such an arrangement?"

"The common word for it is marriage, but within that term, there are so many subsets, are there not? Even if we said a marriage of convenience."

"A marriage of convenience." A loveless marriage.

"If you like, though I certainly think we could learn to enjoy the comforts of married life together. You are beautiful and lively." He stroked the back of her hand with his thumb.

Eliza shuddered and withdrew her hand from his. "But you have more businesslike affairs in mind as well."

"Indeed. I have an old name and an old title, both of which do me little enough good, but they might be appealing to a woman looking to claim her place in Society. On the other hand, you have the financial resources that my prestigious family is not able to leave to me."

"And my dragon?"

"A matter of indifference to me. We have dragon magic in our family as well."

"There are plenty of other rich women who would love to have a title," Eliza said. "Why me?"

"Ah, you wish for compliments? Forgive me, I did not think you tended to that type of vanity."

"All women would like their vanity appeased a little while they are being courted. But I also wish to fully understand your motivations. And I don't wish to be courted simply because I would annoy your family."

"Of course not. You are lovely and interesting. You would not make me a dull or stupid wife, a thing which I could not tolerate. And besides your money, you have connections in the West Indies, a place which I think has more untapped potential."

"I have no interest in returning to the West Indies."

"As you wish. I would not be an oppressive husband, nor tied to your apron strings. Once we had an heir, I would turn a blind eye to any of your activities."

"As you would wish me to do with yours."

"Naturally. We would both be free."

Eliza took a deep breath. Freedom. It sounded so sordid the way Lord Blanchfield laid it out before her. "I thank you for your offer, my lord. I will... think on it."

"Very well. But I will not give you long. I must move forward with my plans, and this offer cannot be wholly unexpected by you."

"No, it is not. Thank you, my lord."

She turned to drift back into the room with the others. Parry stood there, watching her with a reserved concern in his eye. Despite all his interfering, she had still managed to secure her goal: an engagement to a reprehensible man. And possibly even a social situation that would give her all the freedom she could want.

She glanced again at Parry, wondering if he would come to her rescue. He quickly looked away, his jaw tight. He had truly given her up, just as he promised. A lump hardened in her throat, making it hard to swallow. Hard to breathe. What did she want? She touched her reticule, and even through the fabric, she sensed the power of the brooch. Of water, flowing forever closer to freedom, breaking down whatever obstacles stood in its way, no matter how long it took.

She turned back to find Lord Blanchfield watching her, a possessive interest in his eyes. "I know my answer, my lord."

A glimmer of triumph flashed in his eyes. "I did not think you would have to think long."

"I do not wish to marry you."

"You..." His eyes narrowed. "Is this some negotiation tactic? It won't do. I admire you for trying to be clever, but I will ask you to leave the business dealings to me."

"It is not a tactic. It is honesty. Something I know I could not live without."

"Honesty, is it? You want an ongoing accounting of my mistresses and spending? Drinking and gambling? An odd request from a wife, but I'm willing to indulge it."

She wrinkled her nose. "You misunderstand me. I will not marry you. Nothing could induce me to do so."

"Why this sudden change of heart?" His gaze fell on Parry. She did not look, but her cheeks warmed, and she gave Lord Blanchfield a defiant look. He smiled. "Ah, have you let your emotions get entangled? Foolish girl, I had thought you wiser than that. You would not be happy living in a little fishing shack with a broken sailor, now, would you? Better to marry me now and dally with all the captains you wish in the future."

She almost slapped him. Almost. But that was what he wanted—to provoke her. Instead, she did something that would hurt him more. She turned her back on him and walked away.

Parry watched her with sharp interest, and the warmth in her cheeks spread over her face and chest until she felt like she was glowing with self-consciousness. But she didn't look at him, either. Instead, she walked toward the low fire to give her an excuse for the heat flooding through her.

Would she be happy living in a fisherman's shack? Well, it wouldn't be a shack. Parry wasn't that bad off. But if her father disapproved, it might be a rather meager existence. No silk dresses and fine parties. No more always being on guard. Always worrying what people thought of her. And Parry to keep her safe and warm. It might not be so terrible. It might almost feel free. But could she and Parry get along? Did Parry actually want to? Sometimes his flirting seemed in earnest, but at other times, he was withdrawn, just watching her. A guardian. Not a lover. And now, he had relinquished even his guardian role.

Max came trotting into the room, his cravat disordered and his eyes darting about nervously. He made his way to Westing and whispered something in his ear.

Westing's already-pale skin turned almost ashen, and he mumbled something and strode out of the room. Max, still looking a bit stunned, tried to cover for Westing by picking up the conversation with Lady Millicent and Mr. Hackett.

"Now, where did Westing go in such a hurry?" Lady Millicent asked.

Max started and looked over his shoulder. "Er... issue in the kitchen, perhaps?"

Lady Millicent cocked her head. "Wasn't your message the one that drew him away?"

"Oh, yes. Suppose it was. Erm. Kitchen. Yes."

Hackett, who had been listening to this exchange with a dull expression, sized Max up and said, "Are you a hunting man? Seems to me you have the build for riding pretty light over the hedges."

Max stared at him as though addressed in a foreign language. "Um. Hedges, you say?"

"Indeed. I'm a bruising good rider, you see. Not many can keep up with me."

"I should imagine not, if you're riding into hedges."

And the two men eyed each other warily, over a thousand years of the evolution of the English language failing to give them the tools to understand each other.

Blackerby, though clearly amused, chose that moment to slip out of the room. Parry, Eliza realized, was already gone. Well, leave it to the men to desert Eliza and Phoebe with their guests. Phoebe, in fact, had gone wide-eyed, and she wasn't even pretending to talk to Lady Amelia anymore.

"Excuse me," she muttered, and hurried out of the room.

Eliza sighed to herself and then followed after her friend, leaving poor Max to stammer more excuses for Westing's entire party.

Chapter Twenty

ELIZA FOUND the others gathered around Deborah in the garden. "What on earth is happening?"

"My uncle! He's here!" Deborah looked ready to swoon.

"You mentioned that," Blackerby said. "But you have yet to give us any specifics."

Deborah huffed and glared at him. "He and his men are attacking the tor."

"Attacking the tor?" Westing glanced in its direction, but it was a foggy evening and the rise wasn't clear through the mists.

"They're trying to dig or blow it up. We saw suspicious movement, and Mr. Hart snuck over to investigate." She paused for a dramatic sigh. "As soon as he saw the men with shovels, he hurried back to warn everyone."

"Did he see your uncle?" Westing asked.

"No, but who else could it be?"

"She has a point," Blackerby said, his lips twitching in amusement.

"Probably," Westing said. "But either way, we can't let anyone dig up the tor. If our theory is correct, that dragon might also have a magical object."

"Actually—" Eliza began

"Do you have guns?" Blackerby cut in.

"A few hunting pieces," Westing said. "And Parry has a pistol, I believe."

Parry nodded. "I do, but I think Miss Prescott had something to tell us."

Eliza took a deep breath, not sure if she should thank Parry or be annoyed with him. Regardless, everyone was now looking at her. She drew the brooch out. "I believe this is the water dragon's item. I was drawn to it when we searched before. I didn't realize immediately, but it seems to enhance my water magic."

The others stared at her in various degrees of surprise.

She cleared her throat. "So, you see, Shaw won't be able to find it."

"And you think you can use its power?" Blackerby asked, eyes glittering with interest. "Or communicate with the dragon?"

"Maybe you can warn the dragon that it's in danger," Westing said to Eliza.

"Oh, how I would like to talk to one! Like you, Rahab!" Deborah scratched her dragon on the head. "What would you have to say, darling?"

Eliza tried to meet their eyes. "This dragon hasn't been very forthcoming, but I do think I have heard it whispering in my mind. I thought it was the sea. Maybe in a way it was. I feel like my water magic is stronger now. I wonder how separate dragon and element are at this point."

"It's odd, though, isn't it?" Deborah asked. "That a water dragon doesn't live in the water?"

Blackerby looked interested by that. "They may not be able to breathe under water, though there are stories of sea dragons. This one is very close to the sea. And I find it interesting that it seems to have moved into the abode of another dragon, though one of a different attunement."

"Perhaps this stretch of the shore needed to be guarded," Westing said. "Not just by military might, like the Westings, but by magic as well."

Blackerby nodded. "The southern coast has always been

vulnerable, back to the Romans and Saxons and likely before. It was a storm dragon who helped our navy defeat the Spanish Armada."

"Then this dragon may also help us," Eliza said. "I have wondered if that's why it led me to the brooch."

"I hope so!" Blackerby said. "But we won't find out until we go to the tor and drive off Shaw's men. Westing, the guns!"

Westing retrieved his guns and swords and armed the men in a trice.

Phoebe folded her arms. "You can't expect us to stay behind. You need Eliza, at least. And our dragons will help."

"And I want to face my uncle!" Deborah said, putting a hand on Rahab perched on her shoulder.

"Very well," Westing grumbled. "Just stay back."

They hurried for the tor, moving quietly through the fog as they drew closer. Something about it seemed wrong to Eliza. Not just the uneasy feeling she had, but it looked...

"Someone has been digging," Westing said.

"Spread out," Blackerby ordered.

The shadows rolled away from him, blending into the mist to make it as thick as a London fog. Westing raised his gun. His dragon lifted into the air, ready to spew ice at any who attacked him.

Eliza glanced at Amethyst. Her own dragon breathed hot water. And Deborah was attuned to lightning, though Eliza had never seen her or her dragon use magic. What could a full-grown water dragon do? Eliza tried to open her mind, to feel the power of the great waters, to call it to her. The sea was there, but it slithered past her, refusing to come to her call. No, the sea and its dragon would not obey her, and she knew better than to try to force them.

They circled the tor, toward the sea. Their dragons glided overhead. Westing pointed to another spot where someone had been hacking away at the hill with a pickaxe. Eliza hurried over with the others.

"There's no way they can dig through it," Westing said. "If we didn't know Shaw was about, I would say this was just some treasure hunters. It seems—"

"Desperate," Parry said. "He wants to get control of a dragon. He's settled on this one, perhaps because he thinks he can access it more easily than others."

"Well, he won't get it!" Eliza said.

"No, he won't," Parry said.

Eliza smiled shyly at him, glad he was at least talking to her again. She stepped aside from the others, and Parry followed.

"You knew what I had, didn't you?"

"I suspected during the conversation today."

"I wasn't sure before then, either. How did you know?"

"You've always reminded me of the sea, beautiful and untamable. But lately, I can smell the salt air around you, see its light reflected in your eyes."

"It was so obvious?" Eliza felt embarrassed. Had everyone suspected, then?

But Parry smiled. "Only to me, love."

"I think the dragon wanted me to find it. Or, the sea did."

"I have no doubt. Now, does the sea tell you how to protect the dragon?"

"I don't know."

"We're not alone," Blackerby said, his voice carrying through the fog.

"Get ready," Parry ordered in his captain's voice. He automatically stepped in front of Eliza.

Eliza didn't have a weapon, aside from Amethyst, so she just stood straight beside Phoebe and Deborah, prepared to do what she must to stop Shaw. The sea breeze whispered through her hair, pulling a strand loose. She pushed it back into place.

A crack rang through the air, the distant sound of gunfire. Parry drew his own pistol, but he didn't fire yet—the approaching men were too far away. There were many of them, though. A dozen, at least. Eliza looked out to sea, and through the fog, she caught a glimpse of a ship in the Channel. Shaw's allies, no doubt.

Westing gestured, and his dragon shot forward. The ruffians hesitated at Dragon's approach, and it dived down to hiss shards of ice in their faces.

"Go!" Eliza said to Amethyst.

The dragon launched into the air to follow Dragon into the fray. Phoebe and Deborah's dragons glided behind her.

The ruffians scattered, and Westing, Parry, and Blackerby separated to intercept them. Several attackers ran toward the women. Phoebe gestured with her hands as though she were dancing, and a bright light flashed in the men's faces. They howled in pain and surprise and fell back, fumbling blindly.

Then Parry was there, fighting with sword and pistol to keep the men back. His face was set in a grimace like Eliza had never seen.

Blackerby's shadows flew around the melee like a maelstrom. One clung to an attacker, cocooning him in darkness. The man shrieked in horror and clawed at himself as though his nightmares had become real.

Eliza, Phoebe, and Deborah fell back to avoid being caught in the fight. But when Westing joined Parry to make a push against the attackers, it seemed they were gaining the upper hand, forcing the men away from the tor.

"Push forward, cowards!" called a voice behind the ruffians. "Remember what you are fighting for!"

Their leader stepped forward.

"Uncle!" Deborah's eyes grew wide at the sight of the man, and she quailed, her chest moving with rapid, panicked breaths.

Phoebe brought her hands to her mouth, looking about as if seeking an escape.

Shaw fought his way forward. Eliza had only glimpsed him in his previous guise, and she was surprised by how ordinary he looked: medium hair, medium height and build—totally forgettable.

One of his confederates turned to flee from Blackerby's approach, and Shaw shot the man down. Eliza gasped. Not so forgettable, then.

"Death to all who are not valiant in the cause!" Shaw cried.

His men rallied, circling in on Westing and Parry.

Shaw raised his gun at Blackerby, but the earl's dragon swooped into Shaw's face, raking claws across his forehead and chin. Shaw grabbed the dragon, which bit deep into his arm. Shaw screamed and tossed the dragon aside.

"Here's a fact you might not know about dragons," Blackerby

called over the clang and grunts of the fray. "Mine is one of the few that is venomous."

Shaw gritted his teeth. "Press the attack! Death to the dragon masters!"

His ruffians gave a throaty huzzah, and one knocked the gun from Westing's grip. Westing responded with a right hook that leveled his opponent.

Shaw spotted Deborah clutching Phoebe, and a cold grin spread over his face.

"Niece!" Shaw called. "Stop this silliness and come back with me. We are not through with our crusade."

Deborah looked to Phoebe, who put a strengthening arm around the girl. Deborah's expression hardened.

"Yes, *we* are," Deborah said with breathless fury.

She stepped forward, shaking off Phoebe, and raised her arms. Shaw hesitated at the look of pale fury on her face. Her blonde hair moved as if under the power of some mystical wind, tendrils standing out from her head. Shaw's eyes widened, and he put a hand out as if to stop her. Lightning crackled across the sky, striking the top of the tor and the ground in front of the attackers.

Painful tingles raced up Eliza's arms. The answering thunder rumbled in her chest and shook the trees. The air filled with the almost-sweet scents of a rainstorm and something burnt. The flash left Eliza blinking, trying to see anything but colorful streaks dancing in front of her eyes.

The attackers screamed, stampeding in every direction.

"Back to the town!" Shaw called. "They won't dare use their foul magic there!"

"Stop them!" Westing called.

Eliza, still rubbing her eyes with one hand, fumbled in her reticule with the other. She was vaguely aware of the rest of her party rushing forward after Westing. But if there was a time for powerful water magic, this was it. She couldn't control the sea. She had always understood that. But the sea would be hungry for Shaw's ship. If she could encourage it to take it, Shaw would be stranded.

Her fumbling fingers found the brooch, her mind calling out to the mighty, eternal power of the waters for help.

And she couldn't move. She was in the sea. It filled her mouth and her nose, singing through her as it claimed her. She couldn't breathe, but she didn't need to. She was the water now. She flowed, not entirely free, but happy to flow with the currents, the pull of the moon, the flight of the wind, in their eternal dance. She saw before her the cliffs of Lyme Regis. The tide was high, and the water slammed into the rocks. She wanted to claim them, and she knew that someday she would. As long as she did not stop. And she never would. The cliffs pushed back, as they always did, standing firm and solid in the way of earth. But the water found its way in. An opening in the cliff. A cave. A passageway.

Darkness.

Chapter Twenty-One

"ELIZA! Miss Prescott! Wake up, blast it!"

Eliza groaned and opened her eyes tentatively, expecting to see the froth and bubbles of the raging sea. Instead, she focused on Captain Parry's worried face leaning over her. She gasped, sucking in lungfuls of air. She was alive, human, on land. She lifted a hand and stared at her fingers. How odd, to be contained in a vessel of flesh again.

"Miss Prescott?" Parry asked again.

"Captain Parry?"

"Thank goodness you're unharmed. What happened?"

"I was..." She pushed herself up and looked around. "Where is everyone?"

"They followed Shaw to town. I noticed you'd fallen behind, and I found you fainted here. It looked like you were having a seizure."

He gently touched her face, and she did not pull away. The warmth of his fingers on her skin brought her more to herself.

"I was in the water," she said. "No, that's not right. I *was* the water. I think it was my magic. Or, rather, the dragon's."

Parry sat back, and she felt chilled without his closeness.

"Is the dragon trying to tell you something, then? A way to defeat Shaw, perhaps?"

Eliza steeled herself and pulled out the brooch. She closed her eyes. Once again, she saw the waters charging against the cliffs, though this time the magic did not consume her. And as she rode with the waves, she saw it—the way into the dragon's cave. It was so obvious, she laughed.

"The dragon is humorous?" Parry asked, a little impatient.

"Not exactly. But the way in is through a sea cave."

He smiled. "There's sense in that. Is it all underwater, then?"

"Only when the tide is high, I think."

"It is not now."

"Then what do we do? Do we just keep it hidden?"

"I think we try your idea of talking to the dragon. It may know it's in some danger, but it doesn't seem able to protect itself well under the tor. I suspect it's asking for help."

"Then we will go to it."

Parry helped Eliza up, and he kept her arm through his as they picked their way down the cliffside to the beach. Eliza was glad she had not worn a favorite dress, because this one was stained and torn beyond mending. Clouds of mist rolled around them, offering glimpses of their way and then concealing it.

The beach was as Eliza had seen in her vision, or whatever the brooch's magic had showed her. The tide was coming in, lashing the sands, but they could still walk along the shore.

"We'd better move quickly," Parry said, squeezing her arm and pointing through the mist to several figures on the cliffs above. "I think some of Shaw's men have spotted us."

Eliza nodded and lifted her skirts with her free hand so they did not become sodden and slow her down. She broke into a jog, Parry keeping pace with her, but the voices of their pursuers called out of the fog, strangely muffled and directionless.

When the sea wind pushed the fog aside for a moment, Eliza saw dark figures following them on the beach.

"I'm sorry I'm not faster," she puffed.

"I'm no runner, either, love."

"If they catch us," Eliza said, struggling to catch her breath, "We will only have led them to the dragon."

"I know." Parry's face was grimmer than she had ever seen.

He pulled her behind an outcrop of rocks then turned and fired his pistol. Eliza's ears rang at the blast. Their pursuers ducked behind a boulder. Amethyst swooped at them, and they fired off a shot. Eliza winced, even knowing that the dragon couldn't be hurt that way.

Parry grabbed Eliza's arm and hurried her forward.

The men called out and hurried after them, no longer aiming for stealth. They were gaining ground quickly. One of them fired a gun, and Parry jerked, hissing under his breath.

"They hit you!" Eliza said.

"My arm. I've had worse. I don't think I'll lose it." He forced a lopsided smile. "Keep moving!"

Eliza glanced back to see Amethyst harassing the man with the gun, then she stumbled onward, no longer holding onto Parry as he gripped his injured arm with the good one. The sound of the men's panting breath came over the crash of the surf.

Parry stumbled to a stop. "Go ahead. I'm going to distract them. Hold them off."

"You're—" Eliza stared at him. "You're not coming with me?"

Pain lined his face, and blood seeped out between the fingers he held over the wound. "I won't make it if there's any climbing."

"I knew you were hurt worse than you let on."

He smiled then, a little, like the Captain Parry she had known for so long. A smile that possessed its own small place in her heart. "Clever lass."

He turned and shot again at their pursuers, who hesitated, looking for shelter from the pistol.

"You go wake the dragon," he said. "I won't hold you back."

"Oh, you never did!" Eliza said impatiently. "And you understand the sea, even more than I do. What if the dragon won't listen to me?"

Parry gripped her arm with his wounded hand, looking directly into her eyes. "Don't fear its power. Accept it. Let it be what it is." His gaze was not angry, but glowed with a warm, open admiration. Too open.

"You don't think you're going to survive," Eliza whispered.

"Maybe my luck will hold a little longer."

He turned back and fired again, holding their pursuers off a little longer. Amethyst had forced the one with the gun to drop it in the surf, rendering it useless. The dragon flapped back over to join Eliza.

Parry looked again at Eliza. "Though, sometimes maybe I rely too much on luck and don't take things into my own hands often enough."

He leaned in, tightening the grip on her arm, and kissed her soundly. She leaned into his touch, losing herself in the warmth of his lips on hers and the rush of her heartbeat in her ears, drowning out even the pounding of the waves.

When he stepped back, Eliza could only stare at him for a moment.

"Go on, lass! Hurry!" he said with a grin.

"You have to survive," she said, a little dizzily. "So we can do that again."

"I'm very motivated, then. Now go!"

Eliza turned, and Amethyst glided beside her. She wanted to laugh or cry but put all that energy into running. Running away from Parry with the hope that she could wake the dragon before Shaw's men overwhelmed him and that she could kiss him again.

Chapter Twenty-Two

THE ENTRANCE to the cavern was tiny and hidden in the fissure of the rock. Eliza never would have found it were it not for the brooch, and her admirable figure was squashed uncomfortably in wiggling through. A young dragon may have once been able to fit through that gap, as evidenced by how easily Amethyst followed her, but an older, larger one would have to have another way out. Eliza hoped the dragon did. She also hoped she could help the dragon without Parry's sound ideas to guide her.

Perfect darkness swallowed her not far into the cave. Phoebe would have been helpful here. But Eliza shut her eyes and pictured what the brooch had shown her. She climbed forward, letting her mind's eye guide her, not fighting her instincts. Rocks snagged at her skirt and cut her palms. The dank scent of underground filled her nose and her throat. Something else, too. A rich, warm animal scent—strange, but not unpleasant.

A faint glow, barely noticeable at first, let her pick her way more easily as she climbed up. She thought at first it was magical light from the dragon, but she realized the center of the tor opened into several large caverns, and somewhere up above, a gap in the tor let in a faint stream of late evening light. She picked her way through a labyrinth of stone, shadows spreading around her like the wings of ancient beasts.

She stepped into a massive cave in the center of the tor, the dusky light streaming down from a fissure above. What she might have taken for another mass of rock in the path revealed itself into actual wings, taloned claws, and a long neck, all nestled into a nest of rocks. In the faint light, the dragon's scales shimmered with iridescent blues. Whatever color the dragon had been born, only the sheen of its water magic remained.

Its eyes were open. Eliza gave a start and paused. The heavy-lidded gaze appeared half asleep, but the creature blinked. Eliza, uncertain what else to do, curtseyed.

"Do I have the honor of addressing the water dragon of the Dorset coast?" Eliza asked. It felt odd talking to a dragon and expecting an answer, since Amethyst never did more than nudge her ear.

The dragon moved slowly, very slowly. Its eyes opened further and fell on Eliza. Eliza felt a tug from the dragon, like the pull of the tide. She remembered Parry's advice and gave into the pull, stepping closer.

You are of the water.

The thought echoed in Eliza's mind, so loud and direct that it almost overcame Eliza's own thoughts. Like the water trying to pull her under. Then she steadied herself and spoke out loud.

"I am."

I feel it. Out there and in you.

"Yes. But there is danger, too. Can you feel that?"

I know little down here in my slumber, but something has disturbed my rest. A wrongness in the world. Danger to my land.

Eliza stepped closer. "This danger is coming for you. There are men who would capture you, kill you if they can. Is that why you guided me to the brooch?"

The dragon's head shifted, and several dislodged pebbles clattered across the floor. *Yes. I sensed a need.*

"Can you not fight these wicked men?"

One dragon cannot fight an army. We have told the humans of Devon this before.

"The earth dragon."

He was my sire. The dragon body heaved in what seemed like a sigh. *They did not understand. They tried to force the powers of the elements, and it destroyed him.*

"I am sorry," Eliza said softly. "We know what they did was wrong. My friends and I would never try to force you to do anything, but we are willing to help. Anxious to, in fact."

We elder dragons rarely act directly. It is not our place to interfere in the affairs of men. But some dangers run deep, threaten the fabric of our world.

The words echoed in Eliza's mind and sent a tremor through her body. "Is this danger—this man Shaw—such a threat?"

I only know that I sense a chaos hungry to consume light and order.

"Tell me what I must do to stop him."

The dragon rumbled, and Eliza realized it was laughing. *You and I, little human, cannot stop chaos on our own. Not even with the aid of the allies that I sense: light, darkness, lightning, ice. Powerful forces. But we can make a stand for what it is ours. That is all any of us can do.* The dragon shifted again, releasing a tiny avalanche of rattling stones. Eliza feared the whole cave would come down on them, but the solid rock of the fissure held. *The water will help us.*

Eliza looked around. There was dampness in the cave, and a small trickle of water making its slow way to the sea. "How?"

We will ask it to. No one may command the elements, but it will flow to us if we understand it and open ourselves to it.

Eliza took a deep breath, frightened at the thought of letting the water have her. "And we can use it to stop Shaw?"

It is not so simple. We can unleash its power, but we cannot control the consequences. Are you willing to take that risk?

Eliza turned the brooch over in her fingers, considering. If they did nothing, Shaw's men might kill Parry. Her others friends, too. He would unleash a reign of terror in England if given the chance. Better to risk the unknown than the certain devastation. "Yes, I am."

The dragon rose, her great neck high above Eliza. *I sense someone else nearby. An echo from long ago. My sire.*

"The earth dragon? His bones rest near this place"

Yes. His magic was of the earth. When the humans killed him, I left the sea and came to rest in his place. His flesh has returned to its element, and yet I feel something of him nearby.

"There is a young girl attuned to earth who has found him, and the ring that was his magical object."

The dragon closed its eyes for a moment. *He would have liked her, I think. I feel a connection with her dragon. Perhaps it is kin of mine.*

"Can you talk to it?"

We understand each other without words.

"Shaw, the man who is trying to control you, has taken her dragon captive."

We will not allow that. The dragon heaved to her feet and spread her wings like an umbrella. *Come close. You will need my protection.*

Eliza hurried under the shelter of her wings. Amethyst, cradled in her arms, watched with alert interest, tongue flicking as she studied her giant cousin.

The earth trembled, nearly knocking Eliza off her feet. She braced herself against the warm hide of the elder dragon. Showers of dirt and rocks tumbled around them, bouncing off the great dragon's wings. Then light broke through, and the dragon stood, shaking off bits of turf and dirt from her back. A gaping hole in the side of the tor let in a stream of evening light.

Come, human. Onto my back.

Eliza's breath caught, but there was no time to argue. The dragon, whose body was at least the size of the biggest draft horse Eliza had seen, lowered herself close to the ground, and Eliza climbed on. She straddled the dragon like a horse, sitting between two ridges on her back and held on to the one in front of her. Amethyst perched proudly in front of her and flapped her wings excitedly.

The dragon lurched forward with a powerful leap, balancing for a moment in the opening. Her wings brushed more rocks loose, and Eliza had to duck to avoid scraping her head on the jagged top. Another leap, and they were free of the tor. The dragon shook herself clean, though gently enough not to dislodge Eliza.

Mary Anning stood to the side of the tor, her face flushed with wonder and triumph. Max and Joshua were behind her, their mouths hanging open.

"You told Mary to move the earth?" Eliza called

I called her. Put the idea in her thoughts. Normally, I cannot speak to other elements, but she has held my father's magical object, and it opened her mind.

Eliza waved to Mary, Max, and Joshua. Max still gawked, but Mary waved back, and Joshua threw his hat in the air and danced, pointing in excitement at the great dragon.

Then, the dragon spread her wings, a huge span stretching on each side, much wider than the dragon was long. She flapped them several times, dislodging more dirt and dust, and walked to the edge of the cliff. The waves crashed and simmered below, and Eliza could not see Parry anywhere.

Prepare for battle, daughter of the sea.

Chapter Twenty-Three

THE GREAT DRAGON bunched herself beneath Eliza and sprung out over the cliff, her wings spread wide.

Eliza's heart leaped into her throat, and she was certain for a moment they were only plunging to their deaths, but the dragon's great wings caught the sea wind, and they leveled out.

Eliza straightened slowly, struggling to breathe as the air buffeted her. They sailed through the low clouds, which were cold, damp, and scented like rain. Eliza reached out to touch the gray wisps flying past, but they vanished before her fingers.

The dragon circled lower, breaking through the mist and sweeping over Lyme Regis to give them a view of the activity below.

By the beach, Westing's white-blond hair and Blackerby's swirl of shadows made them distinct from the mob of men who were, evidently, brawling on the beach. Blackerby and Westing appeared to be losing, almost overwhelmed by the circle of attackers. But everyone stopped when the dragon's shadow glided over them.

Several combatants—either Shaw's men or fishermen who had joined the fray—screamed and fled, some even dashing into the surf to escape. Men and women who had been watching the battle scattered, some running for cover and others racing to try to keep up with the dragon's path.

But the dragon was much too fast for them. She swooped around, over the water, and Eliza felt her joy at the sight of the setting sun glittering off the waves.

Too long in the darkness.

It was like the echo of an echo, and Eliza wasn't sure she was supposed to have heard it. Yet she also felt the dragon's longing for freedom, and it rang in sympathy with her own.

Then they drew near the cliffs. Eliza made out a figure limping toward Lyme Regis. Parry, alive! She gasped and reached out. As if sensing her, he straightened, and Eliza could see his grin as he spotted them through the tattered clouds. He saluted the passing dragon.

That man is also of the sea, though he does not have magic.

"Yes," Eliza shouted over the wind.

They sailed downward, plunging near the wide expanse of water sparkling beneath them. Eliza's stomach dropped, and she wasn't sure if they would survive it, but she suddenly only cared for the moment. Parry was alive, and she was sailing over the waters on the back of a mighty dragon, her heart beating in time to the steady rhythm of the great creature's wings. Droplets from the spray of waves brushed Eliza's face. The wind and water were part of her and she a part of them.

They quickly closed the distance, approaching Lyme Regis again.

"What are we going to do?"

There is a sailing vessel holding the hatchling dragon. We will invite the sea to purge itself of such arrogant men.

Eliza nodded. It was what she had thought of as well. She felt herself as one with the dragons—Amethyst and the great water dragon. Their desires mingled with those of the sea below. They invited the water to rise and come to them and wash away all the dangers of the men invading their shores.

And the water responded. It drew back, revealing yards and yards of damp sand that had not seen the sun for several human lifetimes. And then far out at sea, it turned, rushing towards the shore. The terrible, glorious fury of nature, coming to cleanse itself.

Ships' timbers groaned and sailors shouted and scrambled as the wave heaved them toward the stormy sky then dropped them into a deep trough, cracking masts and spraying water across decks.

The part of Eliza that was created of dust and not water thought of the men and women on the shore.

"Those people! My friends!"

Those who know the waters will know to flee. Those who are wise will follow.

Eliza turned hot and sick at the thought of the destruction heading toward Lyme Regis—the destruction she had agreed to. She didn't want to be responsible for this. She didn't want so much control. She ducked closer to the dragon. The sea's roar filled her head, louder than any steam engine, as powerful and fearful as God's fist.

The dragon folded her wings and dived, racing the great wave toward shore. She opened her mighty jaws and blasted out a shrieking call like a hurricane's howl. The sound echoed off the cliffs, and some of the distant figures on shore fled inland. Eliza warmed a little, realizing the dragon had taken her fears for the people to heart.

She tried to see anyone she knew, hoping they all had the sense to run for higher ground. There were still some figures scrambling around the Cobb, but even that huge seawall would not stop the fury of the waves.

The sea reached the Cobb and boomed against its solid rock face. The spray of water blasted into the air, wetting Eliza. All noise from below drown in the rumble of the sea meeting the shore. Eliza glanced down into the swirling blue-brown froth. She reached out to the water with a desperate yearning.

Please, save Captain Parry.

Parry knew what it meant when the sea slipped away from the shore, leaving fish gasping and flopping on the sand. He had to get high, and fast. His arm still bled, and he was dizzy with the loss of blood, but he could not stop. Not yet. But climbing those cliffs seemed impossibly steep and high with his leg stump aching and his arm tingling-numb and useless from its injury.

Maybe luck would stay with him.

Maybe it was time for the waters to claim him, take his bones to sleep with the many sailors he had laid to rest at sea.

He would have liked to kiss Eliza one more time. No, many more times.

He scrambled at the steep cliff, trying to find hand and footholds. He realized he was near the place where they had found the dragon bones. Where all this had started. He stared into the partly-excavated skull of the dragon and almost laughed at the sense that they were both trapped there.

"You know," he said to the bones. "I'm a little jealous of Miss Prescott. I would have liked to ride a dragon. I suspect it's even better than sailing, if anything could be."

He jumped back when the skull shifted. Was this some hallucination brought on by his blood loss? Or was the spirit of the dragon emerging to join him for their journey to the next life?

"Captain Parry!" a faint voice called from above. "Climb!"

The cliffside moved. Shifted like blankets thrown off by a restless sleeper. The skull of the dragon broke loose. It slid down and lay there in a heap of rocks and mud, the empty eye sockets staring out to sea. The dirt continued to settle. Into almost a stair-like path up the cliff.

With the breath of the incoming wave on his back, Parry apologetically stepped on the dragon's skull and began to climb.

Chapter Twenty-Four

THE GREAT WATER dragon glided down to made a rough landing on the hills overlooking Lyme Regis. Eliza half-jumped, half-fell from her back, Amethyst flapping after her. She ran forward to stare down at the destruction below. The sun had sunk below the horizon, but enough light lingered to show rivers of water running from the streets back into the sea, and people sloshing between houses to check for the damage. At least the town was still standing. Eliza shuddered and held Amethyst to her chest.

"It's terrible," she whispered.

Power often is.

The dragon's head lowered to the ground, as if weighed down by exhaustion or grief.

The young dragon is free and its captors' ship destroyed.

Eliza nodded slowly. There was that, at least. "What about Shaw, their leader?"

I sense several lives lost to the sea. I cannot know whose. The sea is indifferent.

Several lives. Battle casualties, Blackerby or Parry might say. But what a terrible burden to carry, the weight of those lost lives, even if the cause was noble and Shaw killed or driven away.

And what of Parry? The sea would have taken him no matter how he loved it. No matter how Eliza loved him. He had been down there, trapped by the cliffs where men and women died when the tides came in.

Eliza slowly sank to the ground. It was soggy with the spray of the sea. The water below slowly receded, the hungry sea sucking the water back into its realms. It would claim its dead as well.

Tears ran down Eliza's cheeks, mingling with the salty spray. She wiped them away, the salt sticky against her skin. Amethyst curled in in her lap and licked her chin. It almost broke Eliza down, but everything was still too distant and numb. The tears were some reflexive action to pain she didn't yet understand.

She refused to believe Parry was gone. The very idea wrenched at her chest, like something had been ripped from her, leaving her hollow and raw.

She shook, and the tears flowed more freely.

The great dragon's head swiveled, and she hissed lightly.

Someone is nearby.

Eliza fumbled to her feet, torn between hope and fear. It could be her friends. Or Shaw could have survived. The great dragon was conspicuous, and he might be able to hurt what he could not kill.

But the figures walked out of the gloom were familiar: Max leading Mary Anning and Joshua.

"That was amazing!" Joshua said, running forward. He stopped and stared up at the great dragon, mouth agape. "Can you talk?"

The dragon lowered her head. *Tell him I am sorry I do not have human words for him.*

Eliza relayed the message, and Joshua looked momentarily cast down.

"Can I scratch the dragon's head?" he asked shyly. "Dragon likes it when I do that."

The dragon lowered her head, and when Joshua scratched under her chin, she made a happy grumbling.

No one has scratched that itch since Katherine, my human, died.

Eliza passed that on as well, and Joshua's grin returned. "What did she call you?"

Pearl.

Eliza pulled out the brooch. "And what do I do with this?"

I will take it back to my rest. It reminds me of Katherine.

Max stepped forward. "Hate to interrupt, but what about my sister?" He swallowed, sending his Adam's apple bobbing. "Or Miss Shaw?"

"I don't know for certain, but I think they would have run inland before the wave hit," Eliza's words were heavy. She might never know for certain about Parry, and that would make it all the more difficult. They had never found her mother, after all.

Max nodded.

"Your dragon is free," Eliza told Mary. "I imagine she is flying her way back to you now, and the people who took her won't return to bother you."

"Thank you!" Her face brightened. "I thought he must be all right when I was able to move the side of the tor and then the cliff. I've never done anything like that before."

"Pearl said that touching the earth dragon's ring would change your magic. But why did you bring down the cliff?"

Max edged forward, clearing his throat. "Here's the thing. Wasn't sure how to say it. Captain Parry was down there."

Eliza's heart soared and then fell, and her stomach turned queasy. At least she would know. "Yes?"

"Well, we pulled him up after Mary made a path on the cliffside. He'd been injured. Lost a great deal of blood. I don't know…"

"Is he gone?" The words made her tight throat ache.

Max shifted. "The doctor is with him back there. He's not conscious. He might not—"

But Eliza was running along the cliff's edge, tripping over uneven ground as the darkness deepened. She had to get to Parry if there was even a chance.

A faint glow came from one of the false ruins, and she raced toward it. Smugglers would not be out that night. And, yes, Parry lay on the ground, not moving, the doctor sitting nearby and smoking a pipe by the light of his lantern.

The doctor stood when he saw Eliza, but she pushed passed him and dropped to her knees by the still form.

"Parry?" His injured arm was tightly bandaged, his false leg and eye patch missing, both eyes closed. The breeze from the sea moved his sun-bleached hair.

"Miss," the doctor said. "He's bled a great deal. He has no strength. I'm afraid he won't make it through the night."

"If you think that, then you don't know him. He's the stubbornest man who ever lived."

She reached out to touch his face, chilly, but not yet with the cold of death. His chest rose with a shallow breath.

"Parry! Come back."

Was that a faint groan?

"If you try to die now, I shall... I shall buy all the stupidest, most outrageously expensive hats you've ever dreamed of!"

She stroked his face gently, feeling the stubble on his cheek.

His eyes slowly opened, his good eye bloodshot and blurry with confusion.

"Miss Prescott?" His voice was hardly even a whisper.

"Yes, I am here. The doctor said you have lost too much blood. You must fight to stay with me."

"Tired of fighting."

"One more fight. For me."

"Lost my favorite leg."

"Oh, Parry. I shall buy you a new one, even better. I thought the sea had swallowed you. I couldn't bear it. I love you, Captain Parry. Tell me you love me, too."

"Of course I do, silly girl. But I am your guardian. What would people say?"

"I don't care what anyone says! I'll throw my money in the sea and we can live in a fisherman's shack."

He chuckled weakly, and it turned into a wheeze. "No need. I'm horribly wealthy."

"You *have* lost a great deal of blood."

"Prize money," he said.

She gasped then choked out a laugh. "Well, then you must live, or I promise I will find a way to claim it and spend it all on the most frivolous things imaginable."

"Hats."

"Worse! Lace handkerchiefs. Gaudy paste necklaces. Ugly ribbons."

"Horrors!" His lips quirked in a faint smile.

She took his good hand. "Then you will stay?"

"For you, my love."

Chapter Twenty-Five

ELIZA WALKED with her arm through Parry's. Despite his laments over his favorite leg, he had allowed Eliza to buy him another and was now able to walk well on it, though it had been several weeks until he had the strength to try.

Plenty of time for Eliza to write her father about her intention to marry the captain. Not enough time to hear back, but it didn't matter what her father said. She was charting her own course in life.

They came upon Westing and Phoebe standing near the tor, while Max and Deborah wandered arm-and-arm nearby. Pearl crouched on the ground beside the great rise, a mighty yawn showing off her sharp teeth. Joshua, Jamie, and little Alexandria pointed and elbowed each other with thrilled terror until Lady Zoe hushed them. The younger dragons romped around their elder, some daring to spring onto her back and glide off.

"If you wished to stay awake, we would do everything in our power to make you comfortable," Blackerby said to the great dragon. "We can learn so much from you."

I have satisfied your curiosity, human, but my place is here, protecting my coast.

Mary, who had developed the knack for listening to the water dragon while she held the ancient earth dragon's ring, translated this word for word. Eliza caught the hint of a smile on Mary's lips at delivering the condescending message to his lordship, the Secretary of the Home Office.

"Very well." Blackerby bowed, and his dragon hopped back onto his shoulder. "Then may your rest be undisturbed by further troubles."

The great dragon nodded her head in return and looked to Eliza, who stepped forward to scratch the spot under Pearl's chin.

Thank you for this chance to see the sun and sea again. They will warm my dreams.

"I will miss you," Eliza said.

Yes, but you have your own dragon for company, and I think you will find your relationship with her changed after using the brooch.

Eliza pulled it from her reticule and passed it to the dragon, who lifted it gently with one claw.

"You are ready to close the tor again?" Westing asked Mary.

"I am, my lord." She held up the ring. "With this, I'll be able to make it exact. Just enough of an opening that a little sun will find its way in. And should Pearl ever need to emerge again..."

The dragon lowered her head in acknowledgement.

"In the meantime," Blackerby said. "You will return the ring after this."

"Of course." Mary's eyes widened in a show of innocence, but Eliza knew Mary wouldn't need the ring anymore to find her magical skills greatly increased. Her own had blossomed even when she didn't use the brooch, though she no longer desired to have any power over the sea. It was too terrible a thing to try to control.

Phoebe drew Westing aside, though close enough that Eliza couldn't help overhearing. "It is so strange to think we have known this dragon, and it will be asleep so near, yet we will probably never see it again. Strange and sad."

Westing lifted her hands and kissed them. "We will protect her and she protects us. It is a bond between us. And a way to atone for the mistakes of my forebearers. But hopefully, we will have peace now."

"Only for now," Blackerby said, strolling over to join their private conversation. "Shaw may be out there—we found the bodies of two of his ruffians, but no sign of him. And we still have the problem of a spy in our midst."

"All sorts of spies it seems," Westing said, glaring at Blackerby.

Blackerby smiled. "Oh, come, Westing. If I wanted your secrets, I could have them."

"But not everyone else's?"

"I can't read minds, unfortunately, and everyone has secrets. It's just an issue of discovering which ones are dangerous."

"I thought your dragon poisoned Shaw," Phoebe said.

"She did. But her poison is rarely fatal. More's the pity."

His words left Eliza feeling heavy, but Parry squeezed her hand, and a rush of warmth washed her worry away. Let future take care of itself. For now, she had everything she needed.

Pearl stretched out her wings, scattering the young dragons and eliciting another chorus of appreciation from the children.

I want to soar over the waters once more before I slumber. I understand this man of the sea desired to fly?

Eliza glanced at Parry and told him what the dragon had said. He bowed deeply.

"Fair dragon, if you would allow me a perch on your back, I would be honored."

The dragon snorted. *A flatterer. But because he loves the waters, I am fond of him. You both may ride.*

The dragon crouched, and Parry helped Eliza onto the dragon's back. They made themselves as comfortable as possible between the ridges running down her back.

"Settled, love?" Parry whispered into her ear.

"Ready," Eliza said.

Ready for whatever adventures life brought them next.

Acknowledgments

I drew from several real places, people, and events in this book, most notably the scientific work of Mary Anning, who really was an early fossil hunter and paleontologist in Lyme Regis on the "Jurassic Coast" of Dorset. I have fictionalized her character here, but I thought she deserved a dragon in addition to recognition for her work at a time when female scientists were shuffled to the margins. As always, I have attempted to stay as true to history as possible while exploring an alternate version of it that asks "what if?"

Writing is generally a solo activity, but a great support network makes the process much better. My critique group, the Cache Valley Chapter of the League of Utah Writers, helps me continually improve my storytelling and wordsmithing. The friendship of other writers, particularly of members of UPSSEFW and the Clandestine writers, reminds me that I'm not alone in this crazy endeavor. My beta readers, in this case, Dan, Karen, and Sabine, bring out the best in my books. And as always, I couldn't do this without the understanding, patience, and support of my family. Thank you all!

About the Author

E.B. Wheeler attended BYU, majoring in history with an English minor, and earned graduate degrees in history and landscape architecture from Utah State University. She's the award-winning author of twelve books, including *A Proper Dragon, Wishwood, The Haunting of Springett Hall,* and Whitney Award finalist *Born to Treason,* as well as several short stories, magazine articles, and scripts for educational software programs. The League of Utah Writers named her the Writer of the Year in 2016. In addition to writing, she consults about historic preservation and teaches history.

Find more about her and her books at ebwheeler.com

Made in the USA
Las Vegas, NV
14 March 2022

45641114R00098